DOG IN THE DUNGEON

'Aminta came back! She can't be a stray, she just *can't* be. She's here for a reason,' Mandy said urgently. 'Let's go to the gallery and look at the dog portraits, shall we?' Tilly and James nodded eagerly.

'I think I remember the way,' James said, as they hurried off up the staircase to the second floor.

'Oh, well done,' Mandy said, as James's finger on the light switch brought the windowless little gallery to life. They stood clustered at the heavy wooden door, gaping, as a hundred painted eyes gazed back glassily at them from the walls. Mandy looked along the row of portraits until she came to the one of the deerhound with the distinctive white diamond in the middle of her chest.

'There!' cried Mandy. 'There she is – there's our Aminta.'

Animal Ark series

LUCY DANIELS

Dog
— in the —
Dungeon

Illustrations by Ann Baum

Hodder
Children's
Books

a division of Hodder Headline plc

Special thanks to Ingrid Hoare
Thanks also to C. J. Hall, B.Vet.Med., M.R.C.V.S., for reviewing
the veterinary information contained in this book.

Animal Ark is a trademark of Working Partners Limited
Text copyright © 1999 Working Partners Limited
Created by Working Partners Limited, London W12 7QY
Original series created by Ben M. Baglio
Illustrations copyright © 1999 Ann Baum

First published in Great Britain in 1999
by Hodder Children's Books

A Catalogue record for this book is available from the British Library

ISBN 0 340 73600 3

Typeset by Avon Dataset Ltd, Bidford-on-Avon, Warks

Printed and bound in Great Britain by
Clays Ltd, St Ives plc

Hodder Children's Books
a division of Hodder Headline
338 Euston Road
London NW1 3BH

One

'There it is,' said Mandy Hope excitedly. 'Up on top of the hill.'

Adam Hope, Mandy's dad, flicked on the indicator and slowed the Animal Ark Land-rover to a stop on the side of the winding road. 'Yes, I think you're right,' he agreed. 'Skelton Castle. Looks a bit spooky, doesn't it?' He looked around and grinned ghoulishly at Mandy and her best friend James Hunter. Mandy wrinkled her nose at her father.

James cupped his face in his hands, pressing his glasses up against the car window. 'It does, rather,' he mumbled.

'What an unusual place to choose to live,' observed Mrs Hope.

Ahead of them, the castle loomed majestically from a faint swirl of blue evening mist. Two towered gatehouses stood guard on either side of a massive, heavily-chained drawbridge.

'It's a real castle,' said Mandy. 'I thought it might just be a sort of big, fancy house.'

'Oh, it's real, all right,' Mr Hope said. 'Begun in the thirteenth century, so I'm told, as a baronial fortress, when Skelton Castle would have had a working moat and men mounted up on the battlements.'

'Wow,' said James.

'Come on, Dad! Let's carry on.' Mandy looked at James with shining eyes.

'Are you sure you want to?' asked Mr Hope, in a voice that quavered playfully. 'We may never live to tell the tale of our weekend in Skelton Castle . . .'

'Don't be silly!' smiled Mrs Hope, digging her husband in the ribs with a well-aimed elbow. 'Mr Blaithwaite sounded charming on the telephone. I'm sure he doesn't eat his guests for breakfast or anything like that. He just has *different* taste when it comes to choosing a new home.'

'Well, I'm up for it,' James said seriously, drawing away from the window and rubbing his eyes. 'I can't wait to see inside.'

'Right,' Adam Hope agreed. 'But, while you and Mandy are having a whale of a time exploring the castle, spare a thought for those of us who are here to earn an honest crust.'

Mandy's parents ran a veterinary practice called Animal Ark in the Yorkshire village of Welford. Animal Ark had been recommended to Max Blaithwaite by one of his friends. He had telephoned to ask if they could be on hand when he arrived at Skeleton Castle with his large collection of pets. 'I'm prepared to pay,' he had told Adam Hope cheerfully. 'Whatever it costs. I'm an old fuss-pot, I know, but I'm very fond of my animals and it will be a long and arduous journey for them. I want to be sure they've arrived in peak condition.'

So Adam and Emily Hope had agreed to work at Skelton Castle the weekend that the Blaithwaites and their menagerie moved in.

'It was nice of Mr Blaithwaite to invite us to stay, too,' James said, looking at Mandy. Mandy nodded.

'Mr Blaithwaite has a granddaughter who is moving up north with him,' Adam Hope explained. 'He thought it might be fun for her to get to know someone about the same age. So he said that you and Mandy were more than welcome.'

'And Blackie, of course!' James grinned.

Hearing his name, James's Labrador, Blackie, blinked, his eyes glazed from his long doze in the car. He shuffled with some difficulty into a sitting position between Mandy and James on the back seat. Lifting his nose, he sniffed deeply at the open window. The air was heavy with the scents of summer. Mr Hope turned off the road and through a pair of imposing wrought-iron gates, on to a sweep of gravelled drive.

The castle stood at the crest of a gently sloping hill. As the Land-rover climbed, Mandy could see the clustered rooftops of a small village in the valley below. They passed along an avenue of trees and entered a wood of huge oaks. It was cool and dim in their shade. Mandy noticed a rutted and muddy cart-track that led to the thatched, peaked roof of a small house some distance away.

'Look,' she said, 'over there to the left. It looks like a little cottage. I wonder who lives there.'

'Perhaps nobody. It's a huge estate,' Mr Hope observed. 'There could be any number of dwellings tucked away among the grounds. I expect it might once have been a gamekeeper's cottage, or a hunting lodge.'

The driveway wandered on uphill towards the castle, running alongside a fast-flowing stream that soon disappeared underground, then widening out on to open parkland. 'There's a stable yard over there,' James said, pointing at a grassy area enclosed by split-pole fencing.

'Oh,' Mandy said. 'They must be planning to build something here. Look, Mum, Dad, there are trenches dug into the earth.' Mrs Hope looked over to her left.

'It looks like the foundations for something,' she said. 'Perhaps they're building a wall.' Metal stakes pierced the trim lawn at intervals, a red-and-white rope looped between them to warn of the danger of the metre-wide ditch.

'It's a beautiful castle,' Mandy said, as they drew nearer. 'But it looks a bit sad to me. It needs cheering up.' A tangle of brambles and plants had sprung up in the bed of the empty moat and had reached out to climb and cover the walls of solid grey sandstone. Several of the windows were closed over by overgrown vines.

'Look, James, there are arrow slits cut into the towers!' Mandy said, pointing. James looked.

'I hope we can go up there and explore,' she added.

The engine of the Land-rover idled while Adam Hope weighed up where to park it. Blackie gave a short bark as an elderly man wearing a blue apron came striding out across the drawbridge of the castle, one hand raised in a salute of greeting. He looked a bit hot and harassed.

'Hello,' Mrs Hope called, getting out of the car. 'Mr Blaithwaite?'

'Booth, ma'am,' he said, 'Mr Blaithwaite's butler.' He gave a polite little bow. 'Welcome to you all. Mr Blaithwaite and his granddaughter are expected here tomorrow morning. I'm to settle you in.'

'It's a butler,' James whispered to Mandy. 'I mean, he's a butler. I didn't think anyone had butlers any more.'

'My wife Ellie and I came on ahead a few days ago,' Booth explained, shaking hands with Mr Hope. 'The castle was sold to Mr Blaithwaite with contents included and, as you can imagine, there's a lot to do to make the place comfortable. If you leave your luggage in the vehicle, we will deal with it later. Please, come with me.'

'May I bring my dog, Mr Booth?' James spoke up.

'Ah, yes, I'd forgotten we have a four-legged house guest this weekend. How splendid. Give him a quick run round, then bring him into the kitchen. And, by the way, call me Booth. I prefer it.'

Booth hurried off across the drawbridge and into the castle. After stretching their legs briefly, Mandy, James and Blackie followed Mr and Mrs Hope. Their footsteps resounded on the slatted wooden drawbridge and they had to stoop to enter under the portcullis – the heavy grating that once was lowered to block the gateway to the original fortress.

Once inside, they were led along the dimly lit stone-flagged passages that led towards the kitchen. Booth stepped briskly ahead. He turned this way and that, so that Mandy lost her sense of direction completely. Blackie's wagging tail thumped expectantly against James's leg as he trotted along in the gloom. Then Booth stood aside at a narrow stone-arched door to the castle kitchen, drawing himself up tightly to let them pass. They found themselves in a warm, brightly lit room. The contrast was so great that Mandy had to squint to adjust her eyes to the sudden glare. Ellie Booth looked up from a large cooking range and spread her arms by way of greeting.

'Well, here you are!' she said, as if there had been some doubt they would come. 'It's good to see you all. I've got a meal ready and the beds made up. And *you*, I expect,' she said, bending down to Blackie, 'will want a bowl of cold water.'

'This is Blackie. He's very friendly,' said James reassuringly, patting Blackie's silky head. He turned and grinned his approval at Mandy. It was going to be a great weekend. Ellie Booth had a wide smile and a gentle manner and, judging by the mouth-watering smell in the kitchen, she could cook too.

Blackie, having quenched his thirst, retired comfortably under the large polished wood table and put his nose on his paws with a sigh. 'Sit down, please!' Mrs Booth urged. 'I'm sure you would all welcome something to eat and drink.'

'Wow, what a feast,' James said, as Mrs Booth set out dish after dish of food.

'It is nice to have someone to cook for,' she said, putting a steaming dish of small, buttery potatoes under James's nose. 'We've only been up here a couple of days, but we're already feeling a bit isolated. Oh, the castle is lovely, but it wants bringing back to life! Start, please. Just tuck in.'

There was a platter of cold meats, a quiche, salads, large slabs of yellow and orange cheese and a large crusty loaf of bread, still warm from the oven and giving off a mouth-watering smell. Dessert was a large fruit crumble with cream. Mandy avoided the meat without feeling awkward. Mrs Booth wasn't the sort to be bothered by her vegetarianism, she could tell.

'This is lovely. Thank you,' Emily Hope smiled.

'Skelton Castle *is* in rather an isolated spot, I must say,' mused Mr Hope, looking at Mr Booth. 'Why did Mr Blaithwaite choose it, do you know?'

'Ah, he's one for history is Mr Blaithwaite,' chuckled Booth. 'He's talked of buying a castle ever since I came to work for him as a young man. Now he's got his dream.' Booth looked around at the solid old walls approvingly.

'Mr Blaithwaite's granddaughter is twelve, like me, is that right, Mrs Booth?' Mandy asked, spearing a slippery potato with her fork.

'She's eleven now, coming on twelve. A dear

child.' Ellie Booth said, smiling. 'She'll enjoy having your company for the weekend, I'm sure. And James's,' she added.

'Mr Blaithwaite takes care of Tilly,' Booth said, 'and a fine job he does of fathering the lass, too. She's an only child and needs a firm hand at times.'

'Now, what a lot of nonsense you do talk, Booth,' Mrs Booth responded, chuckling. 'Why, Mr Blaithwaite's as soft as butter, and you know it.' Mrs Booth passed Emily Hope a slice of quiche.

'All those animals . . .' grumbled Booth, helping himself to the salad. 'He'll have to call a halt to his collection soon or he'll have to turn this place into a zoo!'

'The animals are Mr Blaithwaite's passion, first and foremost,' Ellie Booth explained. 'He and Tilly are both mad about any sort of animal, they collect waifs and strays from all over the place . . . miserable, neurotic creatures some of them are too.'

'Have they got a dog?' James asked.

'Had one – up until a year ago. Honey, she was called. A lovely collie cross. She was very old when she died and Mr Blaithwaite was very attached to her. He hasn't wanted a replacement, though Tilly would adore another dog. Perhaps, when they've settled here in the castle, he'll let her have one.'

'They've already got enough animals to be taking care of,' Booth grumbled, though Mandy noticed that he was smiling. 'Everything from a llama to hamsters.'

All those pets! It sounded like heaven to Mandy. She, too, had been passionate about animals as long as she could remember. She had been trying to picture Tilly, wondering what she looked like and if they would get along. 'I can't wait, can you?' she asked James.

'What for?' James was finishing a last mouthful of crumble.

'For tomorrow, of course. When Mr Blaithwaite and Tilly arrive with their pets. I can't wait to get to know them all.'

'Mm, me too,' James said. 'I hope she's nice.'

'Any tea, Ellie?' asked Booth, wiping his mouth with a large linen napkin.

Mrs Booth pushed back her chair. 'I'll make a pot now,' she replied, then looked at Mr and Mrs Hope. 'I expect you would like to see where you're sleeping. And after that, would you like to go and explore, Mandy and James?'

'Yes, please, Mrs Booth,' Mandy said.

James nodded and asked, 'Do you want any help clearing up?'

'How kind, but it's no problem, James, thank you. You run along and have a look around. It's a fantastic place.'

'Um . . .' James began, 'Is it OK if Blackie sleeps with me? That's what he's used to.'

'I don't think anyone here will have a problem with that, James.' Mrs Booth smiled.

'I've brought his basket,' James added.

'Let's go and get the luggage out of the car then, and I'll take you up,' Booth suggested.

'Thank you, Mrs Booth,' said Mandy, standing up.

'That was a lovely meal,' Mrs Hope said, pushing back her chair.

'It certainly was,' Adam Hope agreed. 'Right, lead on, Mr Booth.'

Mr and Mrs Hope, with Mandy and James, followed Booth back along the stone corridor. Booth helped Mr Hope with the few bulky bags and James carried Blackie's basket. The Labrador trotted along happily, his nose twitching as he took in the intriguing smells of the castle. As they came into the hall, Mandy noticed a huge, carved, marble coat of arms, along with several painted portraits of stern-looking people, hung on the walls. She looked at James, who raised his eyebrows. 'Pretty impressive,' he whispered.

'I believe the Skelton family owned this place for generations,' Booth told them, as they began to climb the wide, uncarpeted, elm staircase which led upstairs. 'As the family's fortunes declined, so parts of the castle had to be closed off. Mr Blaithwaite plans to use a core of rooms on the upper two floors only – apart from the kitchen, down below.'

'Have you and Mrs Booth explored everywhere?' Mandy asked.

Booth laughed. 'Goodness me, there's been no time for that. I expect it will take us a week or so even to *find* all the rooms!'

Booth stopped when he reached a half-landing. 'To the left are the main living-rooms. Your rooms are on the right, off that corridor.'

A few moments later, Booth flung open a heavy wooden door. 'Your room, Mr and Mrs Hope,' he announced, putting down the bags. Blackie barged ahead to investigate.

'Oh, it's lovely,' Mandy exclaimed. The large double bed was a four-poster, and above it was an elaborately plastered ceiling. In the curving bay window was a cushioned window seat. Mandy looked out. The garden stretched out below for as far as she could see.

'Right, now, Mandy and James, if you follow me, I'll show you where you'll both be sleeping, then you can have a wander around,' Booth said. He turned to Mrs Hope. 'We'll leave you to settle in, shall we?'

'Fine.' Adam Hope smiled. 'Take care of yourselves, Mandy and James,' he teased in an eerie whisper. 'We might see you again, or we might not!'

'Oh, Dad!' Mandy sighed.

'C'mon boy!' James called to Blackie. Booth led them along the narrow, wooden-floored corridor. 'Miss Tilly was given a choice of rooms on this floor,' he said. 'She chose the one at the end of the corridor with a large window in it. Yours are side by side, opposite hers.'

'It's like a hotel!' said Mandy. 'It's huge!'

'Here we are,' Booth said. 'I'll put the bags in this one, and you can decide where you'd like to sleep.'

'Thanks,' said James, putting down Blackie's heavy basket with relief.

A smooth mahogany wood door swung open and Mandy and James peered in. The bedroom was carpeted in red and it, too, had a stone vaulted window with a wide, cushioned seat. Light slanted in through the cracks in the studded wooden shutters. The ceiling was heavily beamed in the same dark shiny wood as the floor. Booth unbarred the shutter and folded it back. Soft light streamed in. 'This is nice,' James said, grinning at Mandy.

Blackie snuffled about, then climbed into his basket and settled down. Mandy laughed. 'It looks like Blackie has decided this will be your room. I'll go next door.'

'See you later, then.' Booth said, 'Will you be able to find your way around?'

'I'm sure we will, thank you.' Mandy smiled.

Her room was similar to James's, but it had a washbasin and a pretty gilt mirror, and a small stone fireplace, the grate of which was filled with pine cones. Mandy threw her weekend bag on to the bed. 'We'll unpack later, shall we?' she said to James. 'Let's go and explore.'

They wandered from room to room; some imposing, some empty and echoing, some smelling of must and old stone. James peeped in on a small library, in which few books remained; Mandy found a bathroom. The walls were hung with a faded green damask, and the oval bath was carved out of a pale yellow stone.

'Gosh, isn't it amazing?' whispered James.

'Why are you whispering?' asked Mandy, groping for a light switch.

'I'm not sure,' James confessed. 'I feel like I'm intruding.'

'We've been invited to look around, James!' Mandy said.

'Just a second . . . what's in here?' A door had swung open to reveal a narrow gallery of large, ornately-framed paintings. Mandy was surprised to see an array of dogs gazing out at her from the canvases. 'Dogs!' she said wonderingly. 'All dogs.' They were all of the same breed – a big, proud-looking dog Mandy couldn't name. Her eyes roamed round the room, taking in the fierceness in the expression of one dog, the gentleness of another, the unusual markings of a third.

'Wow, look at this one. It has a collar with a metal spike that . . . James? James!' Seeing she was alone, Mandy shot out of the gallery to find her friend tying his shoelace in the hallway outside. 'Gosh, don't leave me by myself like that!' she scolded him.

'You're not scared, are you?' grinned James.

'Of course not!' Mandy said crossly, as they walked back towards their rooms. She didn't like to admit that she *had* felt a little strange in the room with all the eyes of the dogs looking out at her from the walls. 'I wonder why there are so many paintings of dogs?'

'Somebody's collection, maybe? Mr Blaithwaite's?' James said, adding, 'I don't think I've ever been anywhere so quiet!'

'Cheer up,' Mandy smiled. 'At least we'll be in next-door rooms tonight. You can bang on the wall if you like. I'm going to go and unpack now. If we have an early night, then the morning will come all the quicker.'

James shivered, though he wasn't cold. 'You're right,' he said. 'Goodnight, then.' With a backward, questioning glance at Mandy, Blackie followed him along the corridor.

Back in her bedroom, Mandy emptied her small weekend bag and was groping around for her toothbrush when Emily Hope put her head round the door. 'OK, love?' she asked, smiling.

'Isn't this castle wonderful, Mum?' Mandy said. 'James and I found a portrait gallery full of paintings of dogs – all the same type, too. Sort of like a greyhound, but with a thicker coat and quite a lot bigger.'

'Sounds like a deerhound,' Mrs Hope said. 'They're related to the greyhound family, a dog once used for hunting, I believe. Now, let's all get some sleep, shall we? I've got a feeling tomorrow is going to be a busy day!'

Mandy woke suddenly to the inky blackness of her room. For a second, she couldn't think where she was, but the yellow moonlight that stained the sky reminded her. Skelton Castle! It was strange to think of being here, in the heart of a vast, ancient castle.

She lay still and listened. What had woken her? Then she heard it. A thin, wavering howl, long and mournful, wafting on the warm night air. Her heart thudded painfully in her chest and she pulled the blanket closer about her. The noise stopped but, seconds later, she heard it again. Mandy got up and groped for the light switch, then she pulled on her dressing-gown and stepped out into the corridor. She gasped when she saw James's head poking out round the door of his room. His hair was tousled, his eyes big and round with confusion.

'What is it? Did you hear it?' he hissed.

'Sounds . . . weird,' Mandy whispered. 'A cat fight? A wolf, maybe?'

'There it is again,' he said. 'Sounds like a dog.' Blackie was sitting bolt upright just inside James's door. His ears were pricked with interest. He listened intently, his head cocked to one side. Then, he got up and began to pace briskly up and down beside the window seat.

'It's all right, boy,' James told him.

'Shall we go down the staircase and see?' Mandy asked. 'It may be an animal in trouble.'

'That's not a howl of pain, silly. An animal yelps when it's in pain. It might be a dog far off, baying at the moon,' James suggested.

'There isn't a neighbour within miles of this place,' Mandy retorted. 'Unless you count that cottage we saw along the driveway. And if it isn't Blackie, then whose dog is it?'

'So which way do you suggest we set off to find it?' James hissed.

'Oh, you're probably right,' Mandy gave in. 'Where would we begin in this huge place?'

'Exactly.' They both looked at Blackie, who had stopped pacing and was lying down again. 'Listen! It's stopped,' said James, sounding relieved. 'See? Blackie's settling down. I vote we go back to bed.'

'OK. But *wow*!' Mandy said, and let out a deep breath. 'What a spooky start to our weekend at Skelton Castle!'

Two

Mandy was glad when morning arrived. She'd had a troubled sleep and now, pulling on her jeans and T-shirt, she couldn't remember if she had really lain awake listening for the sound of howling or if she had dreamed it. The pale sunlight of Saturday morning came in at the window, warming the room and cheering it, making the strange noises of the night before seem unlikely.

There was a rap at her door. 'Mandy, are you up?' James called.

'Hmm, only just.' She opened the door, then sat down on the bed to pull on her trainers. James yawned. Blackie's wagging tail beat a rhythm against the bed.

'I didn't hear any more suspicious noises in the night, after we went back to bed, did you?'

'No,' Mandy said, smoothing the blanket and coverlet and plumping up her pillow. 'It must have been the wind swooshing round the turrets of the castle, or something.'

'Plumbing . . .' said James mysteriously. 'Probably old pipes. After all, the plumbing was probably installed—'

'James,' Mandy said impatiently, 'let's forget about it. We probably imagined the whole thing, anyway. Let's go and have breakfast. That way we'll be ready when Mr Blaithwaite and Tilly arrive.'

James ran his fingers through his hair. 'Right,' he said. 'You're right. And I'm starving. Come on, Blackie, you can go and explore the garden now.'

Making her way down the curving wooden staircase, Mandy marvelled again at the age of the great stone walls that surrounded her. She was tempted to have another quick peep at the room where all the portraits of the great dogs were hung, but couldn't quite remember where the gallery was. James led the way along the corridor, beckoned by the warm yellow light from the kitchen at its end, and the comforting smell of coffee and warm bread.

'Hello, you two,' smiled Mr Hope. 'We were hoping you would sleep on so we could guzzle your share of the breakfast!'

'Dad!' Mandy said, grinning. 'Wow, look at it all!'

'I told you I liked to cook,' chuckled Ellie Booth, beaming fondly up and down the length of her table. The sight of the red checked tablecloth, baskets of bread rolls and croissants and the assorted jars of jam was certainly welcoming. 'There's eggs if you'd like . . . sausages, bacon . . .' Here Ellie broke off. 'Your mother tells me you don't eat meat, love. That's all right with me, as long as you don't starve!' She gave out a peal of merry laughter. James then dragged up a wooden chair with a hideous scrape.

'Sorry,' he said, sitting down. 'Did you sleep well, Mrs Hope? Mr Hope?'

'Yes, thank you,' Emily Hope smiled. 'Did you? On your first night in a real castle?'

'Hmm,' James began. 'Did you hear anything . . . in the night?'

'Anything?' asked Mr Hope. 'Anything like what? Ghosts dancing a jig?'

'Ah . . . nothing,' he mumbled. 'Just the wind, I guess. You know . . . howling.'

'It was a beautiful, still night, last night,' said Booth, coming into the kitchen with an armful of cut logs for the stove. 'You've been dreaming, lad.'

'We thought we heard a noise – like a dog howling . . .' Mandy said. 'It sounded so mournful.'

Mrs Hope smiled. 'Knowing you two, I'm surprised you didn't go off to investigate!'

'We *sort* of wanted to,' Mandy said, 'but we weren't certain where to begin in this big place.' Emily Hope laughed.

Mandy asked Mrs Booth to name the array of home-made jams. James broke into a soft, warm bread roll with a small sigh of pleasure. 'Blackberry . . .' said Mrs Booth, pouring coffee into Mrs Hope's cup. 'That's marmalade – and that one is . . .' She broke off. The sound of car tyres on gravel could be heard.

'They're here!' said Booth. Blackie pricked up his ears at the sound of car doors slamming and barked, his tail wagging expectantly.

'Oh They're early!' said Mrs Booth, hastily smoothing into place a few strands of greying hair. In the moment's silence that followed,

Mandy became aware of a tremendous noise, coming from the direction of the kitchen window. A spine-chilling squealing could clearly be heard above a background of braying, honking and shrieking. Added to this was the rumble of wheels on gravel and the revving and whining of engines.

'Good heavens! It sounds like a circus arriving!' exclaimed Ellie Booth and hurried out of the kitchen, her husband in tow. The Hopes, with Mandy, James and an exuberant Blackie, followed. Blackie bounded ahead, clattering across the drawbridge, keen to investigate what sounded like a visiting farmyard.

Three medium-sized vans had eased themselves into parking spaces on the gravelled forecourt on the other side of the drawbridge. Their respective drivers were now peering into the interiors of the vehicles at their collective noisy charges. Mandy, and James – his hand on Blackie's collar – grinned at each other in delight, while Booth and Mrs Booth hurried forward with calls of welcome. Mandy was eager to inspect the contents of the three vans, but held back politely until some sort of order had been established. Then, at the crest of the curving driveway, proceeding at a leisurely pace, there appeared an elegant silver-grey Rolls-Royce. Ellie Booth clapped her hands with relief. 'He's here!' she said. 'He's made it.'

The stately car inched forward and the driver cut the engine and leaped out. He was a young man. He wore a peaked cap and sunglasses and looked as if he could have been a pop star.

Mandy gaped. 'Is that Mr Blaithwaite?' she asked Mrs Booth.

'No . . . Mr Blaithwaite and Tilly are in the back,' Mrs Booth smiled. 'That's Jack Stone, who helps Mr Blaithwaite. Lovely car, isn't it?'

Mandy didn't reply, for out of the back had sprung a boy of around her and James's age. He was tall, and wore trainers without socks. His jeans were cut off above the knee and his T-shirt was dirty and rumpled.

'I thought,' James muttered, 'you said it was a grand*daughter*?'

'Who ever heard of a boy being called Tilly?' Mandy said in disgust.

'Hello,' Tilly called from beside her grandfather's car and wiggled her fingers at them, her voice making it instantly clear that she was, in fact, a girl.

'It *is* a girl,' Mandy said in a whisper. 'At least,

she's got a girl's voice. Let's go over.' Tilly had flame-red hair that was cut extremely short.

'I'm so glad you're here,' Tilly said pleasantly to the Hopes. 'Oscar's been giving us a hard time, I can tell you!'

'Oscar?' said Mr Hope, his eyebrows raised.

'My Vietnamese pot-bellied pig. He doesn't approve of car journeys. Glad we're here so he can get out.' She darted down a hand to Blackie, whose tail thumped happily. 'Brilliant dog, what's it called?'

'Blackie,' said James, who, Mandy saw, was gaping rather rudely at Tilly. Mandy nudged him discreetly. There was no need to stare, even though the girl's hair was shorter than James's and she looked as though she had slept in a tree.

'Well, I'm Tilly,' the girl introduced herself. 'I'm glad you two could come for the weekend. Great place, isn't it?'

'Yes, it is. I'm Mandy, by the way, and this is my friend James.'

'Come and meet my grandfather,' said Tilly and she turned away, saying, 'Gramps! Are you getting out?'

A tall, elderly man with lots of white hair eased himself gingerly out of his seat in the back. He was slightly stooped, and leaned on a cane for support. He smiled in greeting, raising his stick, then staggered a little. Tilly put out an arm to him. 'Grab on to me, Gramps.'

Jack Stone was giving instructions to the drivers of the vans, but dashed over to Mr Blaithwaite's side and helped to steady him.

'Thank you,' he said to Jack, 'very kind. How are they all? Arrived in one piece, did they?' Jack Stone nodded and gave a thumbs-up sign. Satisfied, Mr Blaithwaite looked up at the Hopes and Mandy and James, waiting patiently to be introduced.

'Ah, you must be Mr and Mrs Hope! And Amanda, is it? And James? How good of you to come.' He shook hands with Mr and Mrs Hope.

'Mandy,' said Mandy, offering him her hand to shake. Blackie put a cold nose against Max Blaithwaite's hand and he looked down in surprise. 'Oh, hello, you handsome creature. Was I ignoring you?'

James stepped forward. 'He's my dog, Blackie. I'm James. Thanks for letting him come along, Mr Blaithwaite,' he said.

'Ah, one more beastie won't make any difference around here, my boy. Plenty of room and no good carpets to soil. Have you breakfasted? Have Booth and Ellie been feeding you well?'

'*Very* well, thank you,' Emily Hope said.

'Splendid. Then I'll go indoors and refresh myself briefly, if you don't mind, while Jack and the others unload the animals. Would you like to travel down to the yard with them? I'll join you there in time for an inspection. We didn't have any major catastrophes en route but I am anxious, nevertheless.'

Tilly spoke up. 'But you should have a lie-down first, Gramps. Your leg is hurting. You said so yourself.'

'Poppycock, young lady, I'm fit as a fiddle,' Mr Blaithwaite ruffled Tilly's spiky, short hair affectionately. 'Be off with you and don't fuss about an old man.'

'Right-ho, Mr B,' said Jack Stone, who had removed his sunglasses. 'I'll lead the other drivers round to the paddock area and unload the animals now, shall I? I must say they've all calmed down a bit since stopping. Shouldn't have any trouble. So, we'll see you down in the paddock in a while, OK?'

'Well done,' said Mr Blaithwaite, by way of reply. 'See you in a bit, Mr and Mrs Hope. So glad you could be here to help out. Very reassuring. Very reassuring indeed.'

'We'll go along and see them unload, shall we? There won't be any room in the vans for us, so I'll take you through the garden,' Tilly addressed Mandy and James. Mandy nodded. She couldn't wait to see Tilly's collection of pets – and she hadn't even had a chance to ask Tilly what sort of animals she had yet!

Minutes later, they had skirted the great western wall of the castle, plunging down gleefully into the grassed-over moat bed and up the other side, to emerge in a garden grown wild from neglect. Tilly picked her way along a rutted pathway, skirting ditches brimming with stinging nettles and high, out-of control hedges.

'You've been here before,' puffed James, following Mandy. Blackie trotted behind him, his pink tongue lolling. He was loving this adventure.

'Gramps and I spent a day here, a while ago, with Jack. We had to set up a suitable place for the pets to live in, you see. I discovered this short cut to the paddock area. They used to keep horses here, years ago, and there were also kennels used for hounds. So it's perfect for us. Come on, if we hurry we'll be there before the vans.' She began to sprint.

At the base of a gently sloping grassy hill lay a collection of ramshackle old buildings, hemmed in by elm trees stuffed with cawing rooks. There were a few disused stables, painted a faded ochre yellow, and several thatched huts with grass growing on their roofs. The paddock, Mandy saw, had been secured by smart split-pole fencing and a gate.

'Here we are,' announced Tilly. 'Good, isn't it?'

'Perfect,' Mandy agreed, as James inspected a small scratch on the back of his hand that he had got from a bramble. The drivers, with Jack Stone and Mr and Mrs Hope as passengers, soon approached, entering the area by way of a dirt road to the south. They pulled in and parked as close to the various pet enclosures as possible.

'Jack,' Tilly called, 'Oscar first, please.'

'Yep, OK.'

A hush fell over the yard as Jack unhinged a ramp, then released Oscar. Mandy hugged herself with excitement as a very fat, black, pot-bellied pig emerged into the sunlight, blinking his tiny eyes in evident confusion and grunting loudly. His belly swayed as he neatly side-stepped down the footholds on the ramp. Tilly sprang forward, scratched his head fondly, then persuaded him to go into the enclosure with a handful of treats from her pocket.

Jack Stone and the other drivers were unloading each animal in turn. There were five Canada geese, several guinea-pigs, hamsters, a small grey donkey, a llama, a peacock and a meercat, a large glass tank, or vivarium, brimming with Burmese tree frogs and a huge South American iguana.

Mandy and James darted about from animal to animal, exclaiming happily.

'Look, James,' Mandy said, thrilled, 'he's licking my hand!' The llama was as tame as could be.

'That's Suki, she's a girl,' Tilly explained. 'This is Duke, the donkey we rescued from a travellers' site; that's Munch, the meercat . . . oh, and the geese aren't so friendly, so beware.' Jack led Duke into the paddock, and he brayed with pleasure at being out of the van.

'Would you like to help us settle them?' Tilly asked James and Mandy.

'Yes please. We love this sort of thing,' James said cheerfully.

'There's food in each of the vans, Mandy,' Tilly said. 'Could you haul it out and ask Jack where to distribute it, please?'

'OK,' Mandy said happily.

Just then, Mandy heard the purr of an engine and looked up to see Mr Blaithwaite's Rolls-Royce being driven by Mr Booth. He brought it to a gentle stop outside the yard.

'Snatched a lift,' said Mr Blaithwaite, smiling, coming across the yard slowly, leaning on his cane. 'And how are they all settling in?'

'All well, sir,' Jack Stone grinned. 'Oscar's calmed down. He broke free from his container in the van on the way up here,' he explained to Mr and Mrs Hope, grinning. 'Little devil – nearly had the van on its side!'

'He can be very hot-headed, our Oscar,' said Mr Blaithwaite.

'Max Blaithwaite, otherwise known as Dr Doolittle!' Adam Hope laughed under his breath. 'What a collection of animals!'

When each animal had been released into the pen reserved for it, Mrs Hope took up her veterinary bag. 'Right? All safely in residence, Jack?' Jack nodded, securing the bolt on the pen of the geese. 'Come on, Adam,' Mrs Hope said, 'let's begin, shall we?'

Mr Hope began a brief clinical examination of each animal in turn. 'What signs do you look for?' Tilly asked, peering in over his shoulder as he grappled with Munch.

'For anything that might show us that they have suffered stress during their journey,' Mr Hope replied, leaning his forearm across Munch's wiggling neck to hold him still. Mrs Hope ran her fingers up and down the meercat's furry legs.

'No damaged bones,' Mrs Hope announced. 'Mandy, could you hand me my stethoscope, please?' Mandy delved into the bag. She knew exactly what she was looking for, having so often watched her parents work with animals in the surgery at home.

Mrs Hope listened to Munch's breathing and took his pulse. 'Well, you've travelled happily enough,' she told him. They moved on to Suki, the llama. Mr Hope lifted her lips and peered at her gums. 'What's that for?' Tilly asked, fascinated.

'If the gums are pale, it's a sign that the animal could be suffering from shock. But Suki here is in the pink of health,' Mr Hope said. Duke took great exception to having his pulse taken, and butted Mrs Hope with his forehead. 'Duke!' Tilly admonished, 'they're only trying to help!'

Next the Hopes checked the wings of the

geese. Emily Hope's job was to cover the eyes of the birds, to prevent panic and a possible attack, while Adam Hope gently stretched open their snowy feathers to examine the fragile, interlinking bones.

'James,' Mrs Hope said, removing the muslin bag from the first goose's head, as Adam finished checking it, 'could you take a careful look around each of the enclosures to make certain there is no ragwort about that might be eaten by any of the animals? It's the tall, straggly-looking plant with yellow flowers. Do you know it?'

'Yup,' James said, 'I'll go and check.'

'While we finish doing our round,' Mr Hope added, 'will you and Tilly make sure there is clean water in all the troughs, Mandy?'

'Sure, Dad,' Mandy said.

Max Blaithwaite, who had been wandering around greeting each of his animals in turn, came up to where Mr and Mrs Hope were now examining Oscar.

'When you've finished that, would you mind advising on the setting up of the vivarium, Mr Hope?' Max Blaithwaite asked. 'As you know, the temperature and the humidity levels have to be just right for the frogs to thrive.'

'Certainly. I'm just about ready now,' Adam Hope said. 'Oscar is a bit off colour after the trip. His gums are a little pale. Jack, let's make up a deep bed of straw to keep him cosy. Have you any molasses or something like that? To give him a bit of an energy boost?'

'Sugar lumps?' Jack asked.

'That'll do,' Mr Hope said.

'I'll go and get some.' Jack strode away.

'Right, well done, Jack,' said Mr Blaithwaite. 'Now, let me take you and Mrs Hope into this little hut, over this way. This is where we will want the vivarium set up.' He limped off purposefully.

'They're nearly all happily settled. That's a relief,' Tilly said, grinning at James and Mandy.

'How did you *get* all these animals, Tilly?' Mandy asked, watching her bucket fill with water.

'Gramps had some of them when I went to live with him three years ago after my parents died. Then we just kept collecting more.'

'Oh,' Mandy said. She noticed that a shadow passed over Tilly's face and thought better of asking any more questions. But Tilly's face broke into a smile. 'Come on,' she made a fist and punched Mandy playfully on her upper arm, 'Let me introduce Oscar to you both – properly. He's a great character.' She looped her arm in Mandy's. Mandy looked over her shoulder at James and shrugged, smiling. He smiled back.

'Blackie!' James called. 'Come on, boy. We're going in here.'

Jack had broken open a bale of hay and spread it around for Oscar's nest. Tilly opened the gate to his pen. Mandy and James hesitated. 'Come in,' she urged. 'He's harmless.'

Oscar's little ears waggled in earnest as Mandy and James entered his pen. His black snout worked furiously, absorbing the scent of his visitors. 'Crouch down,' Tilly advised, grinning. 'See what he does . . .'

'Hello, Oscar,' Mandy said, kneeling in the straw. Oscar gave a grunt and trotted quickly towards her. Then he leaned his full weight up against her, pressing sideways, and Mandy, completely unprepared, toppled over. Tilly doubled up with laughter. Oscar pressed his slimy snout up against Mandy's cheek and grunted.

'He wants you to get up and scratch his back!' she chortled. Oscar sat down, in some confusion, and peered through his tiny black

eyes at Mandy. James put out a hand and rubbed his fingers up and down Oscar's thick bristly neck. 'His face is all squashed in,' he laughed. 'And he doesn't smell like a pig.'

'Don't laugh at him,' Tilly smiled. 'He's a very sensitive pig, aren't you, Ozzie? He loves a bath. I scrub him with a brush and he sways from side to side with pleasure.' Oscar's charcoal-coloured ears flapped comically as he trotted about the pen, then paused beside Mandy to sniff at her knees. 'He likes you,' said Tilly. 'Here, offer him a treat.' Mandy was still giggling as she held out a chocolate in the palm of her hand. 'Where did you get him? He's lovely!'

'He belonged to a neighbour of ours who had to move house. He wanted to take Oscar to market! Gramps was horrified, so we bought him. He's very tame. He used to come in the house when he was little.' Mandy, James and Tilly took turns in scratching Oscar in the places he liked best, while Oscar grunted his pleasure and swayed his bottom about happily.

Blackie barked his objection from outside the pen. 'Sorry, Blackie,' James laughed. 'I haven't forgotten about you!' Blackie cocked his head to one side, listening. Then, out of the corner of his eye, he spotted a small wild rabbit nibbling at a mound of spilled grain in the yard. He couldn't resist it. He shot out of the yard, yapping with glee, and bounded after it in hot pursuit.

'Blackie!' James shouted. 'Come back here! Blackie!'

Three

'It was a rabbit, I think,' James said. 'I can tell by Blackie's excited bark. He's after it.'

'Oh, poor little thing,' Tilly said. 'Let's go after him. He might get lost on the estate if he chases it for long enough.'

Mandy was just about to say that, knowing Blackie, this was unlikely, when Tilly caught hold of her hand and hurried her out of Oscar's pen. Jack Stone was just coming in. 'What's the rush?' he exclaimed, as the girls squeezed past him. 'What's the rush?'

'Blackie's chasing a rabbit. We're going after him,' Tilly yelled. James began to run after Tilly and Mandy, out of the yard and across the hilly mounds of the estate.

The land was heavily overgrown in parts, smoothly barren in others. They skirted ancient trees, ducking under low-hanging branches as they ran, trying to keep up with Blackie. The faster he ran, the more his pink tongue lolled and the tone of his yapping grew more excited. It seemed to Mandy that she had been running for ages when, up ahead, Blackie suddenly stopped. She and Tilly and James were gasping for breath and holding their sides when they caught up with him.

Blackie was lying down at the foot of a decaying stone wall. It was buckled with age and its ancient stones were home to a thousand varieties of small creeping plant. It stood at about three metres high, too tall to see over.

'What's up, Blackie?' gasped James. 'Rabbit get away, did it?'

'He seems exhausted,' announced Tilly. 'Look at him – he's collapsed.'

Blackie's dripping pink tongue danced about as he panted heavily but he looked extremely unsure of himself, as though he knew something the others didn't. He glanced about him, head low, eyes darting. James stroked his head. 'Hey!' he said, 'There are plenty of other rabbits about to chase.'

'What's behind this lovely old wall?' said Mandy, who had leaned down to scratch Blackie's heaving chest.

'I don't know,' Tilly answered. 'I haven't been this far away from the castle before.'

'Let's walk around it – there might be a gate,' Mandy suggested.

They walked to where the wall made a sharp right-angled bend, then another, until they came to a high double gateway. A closely-woven pattern of wrought iron had served as a climbing-frame for a mass of bindweed and vine, but the gate hung ajar. Mandy squeezed through it sideways and Tilly followed.

'Blackie won't come,' James called, 'He's just lying there.'

'He's tired,' Tilly told him. 'Leave him. He'll wait while we take a look, won't he?'

'Yes, I think so.' James followed the girls through the gate. They stood in surprised silence at what they saw inside the crumbling old walls. Then Mandy spoke for all of them when she said, 'Wow. What an amazing sight!'

Standing with their backs to the iron gate through which they'd come, they saw that the four high walls enclosed a small graveyard. Unlike the overgrown wilderness of the grounds outside, the green summer grass inside had been neatly clipped and carefully tended, so that each of the tiny headstones was clearly visible.

Tilly tiptoed forward, her hands clasped loosely behind her back. She bent to read the inscriptions engraved into the rectangular grey stones above each grave. 'Aminta,' she murmured.

'Fifty little graves,' James said, frowning. 'And one of them is recent,' he went on. 'Look, it's got fresh flowers on it.'

Over in the corner, a fresh heap of earth hadn't had time to attract a covering of grass. The headstone bore the same unusual name: Aminta, and a posy of crisp white daisies lay across the mound, tied with a pale blue ribbon.

'Look at the dates,' Mandy said. 'This one over here is 1900 and I can only just make out this one. Wow – 1732.'

'This latest grave is new,' James said. 'See? Last year's date.'

'Wait a minute!' said Mandy suddenly. 'I remember where I saw the name "Aminta" written now. You know that little picture gallery in the castle? With all the dog portraits? My mum said they were deerhounds. I didn't look very carefully or closely, but one painting I looked at – of a big grey dog – had "Aminta" written underneath it.'

'Hey! That's right!' Tilly breathed. 'I remember going into the gallery when I first came here. All the dogs are called Aminta. It's written under every picture.'

'I vote we leave now,' James said, rubbing his hands vigorously up and down his bare arms. Mandy saw that he had goosebumps. 'I want to see if Blackie's all right. He hasn't followed us in.'

'Yes,' Mandy agreed. 'We could go back and ask your grandfather, Tilly. He might know about the graveyard and the name Aminta – or at least be able to help us to find out.'

'OK,' said Tilly. 'I'm longing for a drink after all that running, and we might have missed lunch. I'm glad that the rabbit got away though! Come on.'

Blackie was lying in the same position outside the cemetery wall, waiting for them. He was no longer panting but seemed dispirited and disturbed. He got up when he saw James come out of the gate, but only wagged his tail once in greeting.

'What's up?' James asked him, puzzled by his unusually subdued behaviour. 'What is it?' Blackie's head and tail drooped.

'He must be tired,' Mandy said, stroking Blackie's ears.

'Or thirsty,' James concluded. 'Come on, boy. We're heading back now.' Blackie walked quietly and obediently beside James as they headed back towards Skelton Castle, each lost in their own thoughts.

They found Max Blaithwaite reclining in an easy chair in one of the living-rooms in the castle, pouring over a sheaf of papers. He had his feet up on a padded stool and spectacles on his nose. 'You're back!' he said, looking up as Tilly burst into the room followed by Mandy and James. 'You've missed lunch. Wherever did you get to?'

'James's dog went after a rabbit,' said Tilly, 'and—'

'Amanda, James, do please help yourselves to a drink,' Mr Blaithwaite interrupted his granddaughter. Tilly went over to a tea tray and helped herself to a glass of orange juice. 'Anyone else?' she asked.

'Me, please,' James said, stroking Blackie's

head. His muzzle was still dripping from the enormous drink of water he had had in the kitchen.

'Gramps,' said Tilly, 'we found the most amazing thing.'

'What sort of thing?'

'A graveyard!' Mandy burst out. 'We think it's a graveyard for *dogs*.'

Max Blaithwaite removed his glasses and crossed his feet at the ankle. 'Dogs, eh?' he mused. 'How did you come to that conclusion?'

'The gravestones are tiny,' James explained. 'Each of them has the name "Aminta" carved into it, and a date.'

'All different dates,' Mandy added.

'Gramps,' Tilly said excitedly, 'do you remember the gallery of paintings upstairs? All those pictures of dogs, all of them with little brass name plates underneath? All of them – the dogs I mean – called Aminta!' Tilly finished triumphantly.

'Yes,' Mandy confirmed. 'Isn't that a coincidence, Mr Blaithwaite? And quite creepy . . .'

'And one of the gravestones had quite a recent date – last year – and the earliest one was 1732 – though it's quite faded.' James added. Tilly was drinking her juice while walking round the room.

'Do sit down, my dear,' Mr Blaithwaite told her, covering his eyes with a weary hand. 'Are you sure? I mean, I had no idea there was a graveyard on the estate! Why hasn't anybody told me, I wonder? Whereabouts did you find it?'

Tilly explained the direction they had followed in their flight after Blackie. Max Blaithwaite then got up with difficulty and limped over to a pile of papers that lay on a polished mahogany desk. He began to shuffle through them, humming softly as he did so.

Mandy took the opportunity to look around the room. It, too, had floors of polished dark wood. They were so shiny that Mandy could see the arched, mullioned windows reflected in them. Heavy oak beams supported the ceiling. A huge stone fireplace had seats on either side of the grate and there were winged dragons carved into the stone mantel.

'Here we are,' Max Blaithwaite was saying. 'This is the map of the whole area that was given to me by the Land Registry office. Ah, now here – do you see this dotted black line running across here?' Mandy, James and Tilly, who had crowded around the map, nodded. 'That's the line of sub-division. It's a public right of way, and all the land on the other side of it – presumably where you have been today – is not land that belongs to me.'

'That's the land that has been sold off?' Tilly asked, wrinkling her nose. 'All that?'

'We saw that a trench had been dug, and roped off, when we arrived,' James said, remembering.

'Indeed,' said Mr Blaithwaite. 'So, whatever it is you have come across is the concern of one Mr Peter Weeks, a London-based property developer who, I believe, intends to build six luxury homes on that land, turning it into a private estate.'

Mandy was aghast. 'But what about all those gravestones? Surely he can't just wrench them up out of the ground?'

'I'm afraid that's not business for you, dear child,' Max Blaithwaite looked gently at her.

'Well, somebody around here cares about those graves,' James spoke up. 'The grass has been clipped and the place well cared for.'

'Perhaps someone from the village has wandered up from time to time . . .' Mr Blaithwaite trailed off.

'Fresh flowers have been laid on the most recent grave,' Mandy said sadly.

Mr Blaithwaite was studying his map again. 'I can't understand quite why this graveyard you speak of doesn't appear on this map. If you say that it dates from around the time the castle was built, it certainly would be an important historical feature of the estate.'

'We'll go back and take another look . . .' Tilly began, jumping up.

'Now, you'll do no such thing!' Max Blaithwaite said sternly. 'Tilly dear, I beg you not to go dashing about in places where you are not wanted. We have plenty of land of our own and enough to do to keep us occupied on it. Technically, you will be trespassing if you stray on to Mr Weeks's land. Now, let's put the matter behind us, shall we?'

Tilly blinked at her grandfather. 'Yes, Gramps,' she said, sounding disappointed. Mandy was relieved when Jack Stone appeared in the doorway with her parents. The atmosphere lifted.

'Ah, hello there, Mr B,' Jack began. 'Bad news, I'm afraid.'

'Ah, Jack! Adam and Emily!' Mr Blaithwaite greeted them warmly. 'What is it?'

'Oscar's done a runner, Mr B.' Jack shuffled from foot to foot, looking crestfallen. 'Pen wasn't secure. He's been mean-tempered lately, as you know.'

'What?' shouted Tilly, and then covered her mouth with her hands. 'My poor Ozzie!'

'I'm sure he won't go far,' Adam Hope said quickly. 'He's not a very well pig at the moment. Anyway, we've come back to organise a search party.'

Tilly jumped up. 'Quick! James, Mandy, let's go' she begged. Blackie stood up and barked loudly, responding to the tone of urgency in Tilly's voice.

'Booth will help, too,' Mr Blaithwaite suggested. 'I'll be down shortly to lend a hand. Oh dear, oh dear, this *is* a bad start.'

'Sorry, Mr B,' mumbled Jack.

'Just one of those things, Jack ... Arm yourselves with Oscar's favourite treats – celery, apples and chocolates – and let's put in a thorough search, shall we?'

'Right away, Mr B,' Jack said, standing to attention. 'Better leave Blackie up here, James, if you don't mind, lad. We don't want *him* joining in the chase now, do we?'

* * *

Tilly, who seemed to do everything in a hurry, had already sped down into the moat and vanished up the other side, calling: 'Come on, you two!'

Down in the yard, she, James and Mandy briefly inspected the damage Oscar had done to escape from his pen. 'Look at that! He's dug right under the wire – a proper little escape artist,' James said admiringly.

'I thought he might be somewhere inside the yard helping himself to whatever snack he could find,' Jack said, scratching his head, 'but he's nowhere to be found around here.'

'As I said, he won't have got far,' Mr Hope said reassuringly. 'Pigs don't move very quickly.'

'Yes,' Emily Hope agreed. 'He's more likely to amble along looking for food.'

'Still, there's no time to waste,' Mandy urged. 'Let's spread out and search.' Jack nodded. He seemed worried. 'Right. Thanks, gang.'

'If anything's happened to that pig . . .' Tilly mumbled, taking Mandy's arm.

'We'll find him, I'm sure,' James said cheerfully.

'Mum and I will set off in this direction,' Adam Hope said, taking charge, 'Jack, Mr Booth, you head off that way and Mandy, with

James and Tilly, try the woods. OK?'

They went together into the thickets of trees – birch, Scots pine, elm, hazel, oak and holly – stooping occasionally to gently part the bushes, in the hope that Oscar might have taken refuge there. 'Oscar . . . here, boy,' Tilly called, and then whistled loudly. 'Stand still and be quiet,' Mandy suggested. 'We might hear him rooting about in the undergrowth.' They stood statue-still, hoping. 'Nothing,' Tilly mumbled. She looked miserable. Mandy put an arm round her shoulders and they trudged on.

The sun had begun to slide below the horizon when James suggested they turn back and, wearily, Tilly and Mandy agreed. Mandy was worried about Oscar but she tried to be optimistic and bright, for Tilly's sake. They turned back towards the stable yard.

'Any luck?' Mandy asked Jack hopefully, when they reached the yard.

'No, and it's getting on towards dusk. We'll have to continue our search tomorrow. We've left a trail of food for him to follow. He might come back on his own.'

Tilly sniffed, and Mandy could see she was fighting tears.

'I'm sure he will,' she said, hugging Tilly. 'Try not to worry. We're all tired and it's been a day of running about.'

'I'm starving,' James announced, rubbing his eyes. 'We didn't have any lunch!'

'We're going to call off the search, for now,' Mr Hope said, striding into the yard. 'Look, Oscar should come to no harm overnight,' he said, trying to reassure Tilly.

'He's having a small adventure of his own, Tilly. I shouldn't worry,' Emily Hope said kindly. 'And I don't know about any of you,' she added, resting her back against a split-pole fence, 'but I'm ready for a nice hot bath!'

Jack Stone shrugged. He sighed and Mandy could tell he was deeply concerned. 'Yeah, whatever,' he said, taking off his cap and rubbing his eyes. 'I'll go and report to Mr B.'

Tilly's face had been a picture of misery as they had trooped forlornly back to the castle. She had shown no interest in Mandy's suggestion that they go and find the room in which the dog paintings were hanging.

'Try to look on the bright side,' Mandy had said, 'Dad says he'll find his way back home, and the estate *is* fenced – he can't have gone terribly far.'

Tilly had shrugged and given a half-smile, mustering her courage. Then, suddenly, she had brightened. 'I know! Let's have a midnight feast tonight!' James and Mandy looked at each other doubtfully, surprised by her lightning change of mood.

'No, honestly,' Tilly insisted, 'I'll plan it and organise it. It will be fun – and it will take my mind off Oscar.'

Now, Mandy and James were sitting cross-legged on Tilly's bed, facing each other over a tray of treats neither of them could face eating. Ellie Booth had produced a hearty supper just two hours before – and James hadn't been able to resist a huge second helping. There had been plenty to eat, especially as Mr Blaithwaite had not appeared for the meal, sending a message through Booth to say he would be retiring early.

'Try one of these biscuits with chocolate spread on it,' said Tilly with her mouth full. She sat on a cardboard box, as yet unpacked, and behind her on the stone window ledge the flame of a single candle flickered in the draught from the open window.

'Not for me, thanks,' said Mandy, patting her tummy. 'I'm stuffed. But Blackie's keen.'

Blackie's eyes were bright in the candlelight as he gazed longingly at the plate of sugary biscuits and small iced cakes on the bed. He swallowed and licked his lips. Then, suddenly, his ears shot up in concentration and he cocked his head to listen intently to a sound they hadn't heard. James held out a biscuit to him, but Blackie was completely disinterested. He went to the window, sniffed up at the night air, then began to pace, just as he had done the previous night.

'Oh, no,' groaned James. 'Here we go again.'

'What?' asked Tilly.

'Listen!' Mandy said urgently. 'The howling . . .'

The high, mournful wail rose, it seemed, from the very depths of the castle and hung, quivering, in the night air. Tilly shot off her box, spilling her hot chocolate, and went to the window.

'A wolf!' she said triumphantly, leaning out. 'It must be! How great!'

'Must it?' James whispered. 'Here – I mean – in the castle grounds? Wild?'

'It can't be a wolf, just strolling around like that,' said Mandy. The animal howled again. This time the hair on Mandy's arms stood up and prickled. 'James and I heard it last night. Before you and your grandfather arrived.'

'Really?' said Tilly and she dug into a bag and pulled out a woolly jumper. 'Let's go and investigate,' she added decisively. 'Come on, we have to find out what's making that racket. After all, if it *is* a wolf, it might eat Oscar!'

Four

'Do you think we should?' James asked, glancing up at the window. It was pitch black and the castle was eerily quiet, except for the persistent howl of the unknown animal.

'Come on, James,' Tilly pleaded, blowing out the candle and snapping on the electric light. 'This is a great adventure. We won't come to any harm.'

Mandy stood up and pulled on her shoes. 'Well, I'm more *worried* about that poor creature out there than frightened. It sounds as though it might need help to me. Come on, James. If we go together with Blackie, we'll be fine – we've got to find out what it is!'

'I was hoping,' mumbled James, getting up reluctantly, 'that we wouldn't hear it tonight . . .' He looked across at Blackie, pacing up and down below the window, looking unusually nervous. He began to pant slightly. Mandy hadn't seen Blackie this way before. He was usually game for anything and more than eager for a challenge.

'It's not that I don't want to investigate, it's just that Blackie seems so . . . uncertain . . . as though he knows something, somehow, that we don't,' James explained.

Ignoring James's protestations, Tilly produced a powerful torch from the depths of a grubby-looking rucksack. She put a finger to her lips and opened her bedroom door, which creaked alarmingly. Mandy, James and Blackie followed her out. Their rubber-soled trainers were soundless on the wooden floors as Tilly led the way to the top of the staircase. Blackie slunk along beside them, walking as though he expected the floor under him to cave in at any moment. He seemed unusually reluctant.

'Why not take him back to the room?' Tilly said in a hushed voice. 'He's going to wake the whole place with those tip-tapping claws of his.'

James reluctantly did as Tilly suggested,

shutting the door on Blackie, saying, 'You'll be better off in there, boy, I'm sure.'

Mandy walked silently behind Tilly, glancing at the distorted shadows dancing on the walls in the light of her swinging torch. They found a light burning in the hall at the base of the stairs but Tilly plunged on excitedly, into the dark passage and beyond. Twice she paused, listening for the sound of howling, following it for clues to its source.

'It's coming from below us!' James whispered.

'There is a door to the side of the kitchen and I know a flight of stairs leads to what my grandfather *thinks* is a cellar,' Tilly said. 'We'll try there.'

Mandy couldn't tell if she was terrified or excited, but her heart pounded steadily as James and Tilly applied their combined weight to the heavy wooden door. The moment it opened, the sound of the animal howl could be heard loudly and clearly. 'Howooooo . . .' It came floating up the stairs, echoing around the walls, as though someone had suddenly turned up the volume on a radio.

'Somebody,' whispered James, 'is having us on. This is a joke . . . there simply *can't* be an animal stuck down here!'

But James was whispering to Tilly's retreating back. She was already leaping down the stairs in great excitement. Mandy noted how fearless her new friend was and, ignoring her own rising nervousness, followed quickly after her, with James on her heels.

At the bottom, the beam of Tilly's big torch showed a small, unused room, empty of furnishings, except for a large, carved wooden chest. It smelled dusty and musty and made Mandy cough. Tilly swivelled the beam slowly around the bare stone walls. The howling had stopped.

'Are we dreaming, or what?' Tilly said softly.

There, in a corner, an enormous dog was sitting calmly and expectantly on the floor. It had the same smallish head and elegant body of a greyhound, only quite a bit larger, and with a thick, ragged coat of the palest blue-grey. It sat still, gazing at Mandy, James and Tilly with a sort of quiet dignity. It seemed to be measuring them up.

'A deerhound!' Mandy breathed.

'How on earth did it get down here?' Tilly said, amazed.

'Who can it belong to?' James whispered.

'It looks just like the dogs in the paintings!'

Mandy said, 'It's one of the Aminta dogs!'

'Well, it isn't going to attack us, that's for sure. It looks as gentle as a lamb. I wonder how long it's been trapped down here?'

'Can't have been long. It doesn't look terribly thin or anything,' James observed. 'Perhaps it belongs to someone who keeps it in here and comes to feed it.'

'That's cruel!' Mandy said. She moved past Tilly and cautiously took a step towards the dog. But nothing about the great dog's expression or behaviour seemed threatening. It didn't get up, or growl, or bare its teeth.

'Hello, you lovely thing,' Mandy spoke gently, and held out her hand. The dog stood up, and took a step backwards. Mandy saw that it had a snow-white mark in the shape of a diamond on its chest. 'We're not going to hurt you,' she told it, softly. 'Come on and say hello. Good boy . . . girl . . .'

'Definitely mysterious,' James said. 'I mean, it's not frightened or angry, it isn't wounded or sick – so what's it doing sitting down in this chilly old room making all that noise?'

The dog took a few steps towards the wooden chest. It moved gracefully, almost as though it were gliding. Again Mandy reached out,

shuffling slowly forward on her haunches, a
hand outstretched. 'Here, boy . . .' But again the
dog moved back a pace out of Mandy's reach,
still looking steadily at her.

'I can't see a water bowl or any food about,
can you?' Tilly asked, flicking her torch round
the corners of the room. The dog now began
to snuffle, then paw at the wall against which
the big chest was standing. It looked up at
Mandy and cocked its head, then pawed at the
wall again, making a scraping on the stone
with its claws that made Mandy's hair stand on
end.

Tilly crouched low and aimed the beam of
her torch on the dog. 'It's a girl dog,' she
announced. 'Anyone can see that.'

'She doesn't want us to touch her, but . . . I
think she's asking us to open this chest!' Mandy
guessed.

James came forward. 'Shine your torch on the
bolt, Tilly.' He bent down and examined it.
'Hmm, it's padlocked – no hope of opening it.'
The dog had backed off into the shadows when
James had approached. Now she came slowly
forward, put out her elegant front paw and
scraped at the wall again.

'No, she wants us to shift it!' cried Tilly. 'Let's

move it over – she's lost a ball or something behind it, I'll bet.'

James pushed hard against the chest with his forearms. It gave easily, sliding along on the smooth stone floor. 'Look!' breathed Tilly. 'There in the wall!' A small, bolted opening about one metre square had been revealed.

James tugged at the bolt, working it back and forth until it shot free with such force that it knocked him back on to his bottom. Laughing, Mandy and Tilly helped him up. 'Wow,' he said. He turned round to look up at Tilly. 'Perhaps we ought to get your grandfather, or someone.'

'No, not yet,' Tilly said. 'I vote we go in and take a look.'

'Shine your torch over there first, Tilly,' said James. 'Let's see where the dog is . . . oh, look, she's gone. She's gone through the door.'

'She couldn't have, James,' Tilly said. 'The door isn't even properly open yet.' The unbolted door had swung open only a few centimetres. She shone the torch round the room, directing its beam into all the corners. The dog had gone.

'This is . . . *weird*,' said James, with a shudder.

Tilly was on her hands and knees, the metal

casing of her torch ringing on the stone. She had pulled open the doorway and was starting to crawl through it. Her voice came back to them from the other side of the wall, sounding as though she was speaking with tissue paper in her mouth. 'She's here waiting for us. Come through. Oh! It's a dungeon!'

Mandy and James had been plunged into sudden and complete darkness.

'I'm on my way,' James said quickly and dropped to his knees. Mandy followed, groping her way behind James.

The stone was so cold it felt slimy. Mandy could hardly believe she was slithering through an ancient opening in the basement of a creepy castle in the middle of the night, scrabbling after a mysterious dog that didn't seem to be real. She wondered briefly if she might be dreaming, then, as she struck her shoulder hard on the frame of the doorway, realised she was wide awake.

James was sitting just inside the small opening, hugging his knees. It was extremely cold. The room was small and square-shaped, and made entirely of stone.

'Gosh,' James breathed, and a cloud of condensation rose around him from his own warm breath. 'It's a real dungeon . . . where they used to keep *real* prisoners!' Mandy stared about her. Metal rings were bolted into the stone of the wall. James raised his arms and slipped both wrists into the shackles, and hung there with his chin on his collar bone.

'Ugh! James, don't!' Mandy begged.

'Please, James,' Tilly said. 'Where's the dog?' She moved her torch beam away from the gruesome sight of James.

The dog had retreated to a shadowy corner of the room they were now in and, to Mandy, seemed to be waiting patiently for their next move.

'Just look,' Tilly cried. 'Look at all these old books and things here on this shelf.' James began to cough as what might be centuries of pale dust was disturbed by Tilly's searching hands. 'Maps . . . recipes . . . all in funny old writing – marvellous, heavy old books all bound in leather. How amazing!'

'Tilly,' Mandy said softly, 'let's follow her, shall we? There'll be a chance to look at those some other time . . .' Mandy pointed to the dog, who was now standing with her back to them, staring into the gaping mouth of an arched doorway, the metal-barred gate of which hung open. As

Mandy spoke, the dog slowly turned her small head in their direction, then looked back into the passageway and stepped purposefully into darkness.

James scrambled to his feet. 'Oh, quick, let's not lose her now,' he said.

'She wants us to follow her, I'm sure of it,' Mandy said. 'She seems to be taking us somewhere!'

Reluctantly, Tilly moved away from the shelf of treasure and pointed the torch beam in the direction the dog had taken. Mandy suddenly couldn't bear the thought of not knowing where the beautiful creature had come from, or where she was going. She and James ran into the passage beyond the doorway, Tilly close behind them. They trotted after the dog who moved quickly ahead of them, looking back over her shoulder from time to time to make sure they were following.

On and on they went. The rough and uneven stone floor of the tunnel made the going difficult, and twice Mandy stumbled. James, in the lead, now held the torch, which threw out an arc of light showing a damp, moss-covered ceiling. Runnels of water darted and dripped down the walls. They walked downhill for some way, then the tunnel floor evened out for a time before it rose steeply uphill.

'We must be going under the castle moat,' Tilly said, her voice echoing eerily.

'We must be crazy, doing this,' James said. 'We might be getting ourselves into some unforeseen danger and . . .'

'Oh, don't, James,' begged Mandy. 'Don't spoil it. It seems this dog has a mission of some kind. She wants to share it with us. We can't let her down. And, after all, we have come this far.'

'S'pose so,' stuttered James, through chattering teeth.

Up ahead of them, a warm glow of yellowy moonlight was creeping into the tunnel mouth.

'Look!' said Mandy. 'It's moonlight – it must be where the tunnel comes out.' They hurried on to the tunnel's end. Mandy was eager to see if the dog would be waiting for them.

'Oh,' she said, 'Look where we are – again! Back in the cemetery! Well, for heaven's sake . . . all this way and all this trouble . . .'

Outside, the sky was velvet dark. The brilliance of a huge yellow moon meant James could switch off the torch and save the batteries for their long return journey. They stood gazing about them, at the neat rows of tiny gravestones, lost for words.

'Why did she bring us here?' Mandy whispered. 'Where has she gone to?'

Then the dog appeared at the iron gates to the cemetery, her long curved tail moving slowly from side to side. Once more she turned about and headed off into the darkness.

'Oh no,' groaned James, 'surely she doesn't expect us to go farther?'

'Yes, she does,' Mandy said firmly. 'And I'm going to follow, that's for sure. Coming?'

Five

Gusts of wind blew through the high, dark trees. Mandy was pleased to be out of the tunnel and into the fresh, moonlit night air. She inhaled deeply, wondering briefly how moles could bear to be shut away in the earth for such long stretches of time.

'You know,' said James, 'that we are now trespassing on the area of land your grandfather said had been sold off.'

'We won't tell him,' Tilly said quickly. 'It would only worry him, so we won't say anything. Let's just keep this a secret for now, shall we?'

'Yes,' Mandy agreed. 'I think we should. Come *on*, you two, the dog's still waiting for us to follow. Look at her!' Tilly and James looked over to where the dog waited patiently before the gate, her back to them. Occasionally, she glanced at them over her shoulder. In the dark, with the tree shadows dancing across her coat, she looked almost unreal.

'Right,' said Tilly, 'let's go.' She marched forward and, immediately, the dog slithered gracefully through the iron gates. James yawned a great, gaping yawn.

'How can you be tired, James, at a time like this?' Mandy wondered.

'Well, maybe because it's about one o'clock in the morning,' James retorted. Then he went on: 'You know, Mandy, maybe this dog is just a stray. She wandered into the castle by mistake and now wants to go home.'

'If she were a stray,' Mandy reasoned, 'I don't think she would have been quite so aloof. She would have been much more needy, and nervous. No, it's almost . . . almost as if she had been *expecting* us. Calling for us.'

'Weird,' James said again. He switched on the torch. They had entered a shallow copse of oak and beech trees that shielded them from the moonlight. Mandy could only just make out the shape of the dog ahead, moving like a streak of smoke through the trees. She wasn't like a normal dog, Mandy thought. She didn't bark or whine or fuss or leap or even wag her tail as most dogs did. She was patient and dignified and . . . different.

Stepping clear of the copse, Mandy turned to see Skelton Castle on the hill, huge and pink-looking in the moonlight, pale against a frame of black night.

'Can you see her?' Mandy whispered to Tilly.

'No, and heaven knows where she's brought us. I mean, where in the world are we now?'

'Listen!' James had clutched Mandy's arm to stop himself from stumbling over a stone. 'It sounds like water.'

'We're near the lake!' Tilly said, dumbfounded. 'She's brought us to the lake. I saw it marked on Gramps's map.'

Mandy screwed up her eyes in the half-light for a sign of the dog but there was no clue to her presence now. Suddenly, a plaintive squealing sliced through the silence of the night and made Mandy jump. Tilly clutched Mandy, who clutched James, and they stood dead still to listen. There was the sound of gentle lapping, and a squelching, like somebody in Wellington boots walking through mud.

'Oscar!' shouted Tilly. 'It's Oscar! Come on.' She raced away across an expanse of scrubland, over the rise of a hillock and down to where the lake lay, still and inky-black. Mandy and James scrambled after her. The squealing, now accompanied by frantic sucking sounds, got louder.

'Give me the torch, quick,' Tilly commanded. The beam of yellow light picked out the reflections of the trees wavering in the breeze beyond the shore, and Oscar, up to his shoulders in thick, oozing mud. His stubby snout worked frantically as he snorted and squealed in terror, his tiny piggy eyes wild with the effort of his struggling. 'Oh, Ozzie!' said Tilly, her voice filled with tearful relief. 'You silly, silly old pig! Just look at the state of you.' At the sound of her voice, Oscar stopped struggling and slumped back into the unpleasant-smelling silt.

'I'm so glad we've found him,' Mandy said, wrinkling up her nose.

'He's well and truly stuck,' James observed. 'Poor Oscar. Who knows how long he's been battling in that smelly stuff!'

'We've got to get him out,' Tilly said, then added: 'It's all right, boy, we're right here on

the shore. We'll help you.' Tilly flashed the
torch beam about, looking for inspiration. The
torch picked out a boat jetty, standing tipsily in
the mud on tilting wooden stilts.

'He must have trotted along the jetty from
the shore and fallen through.' Mandy said. She
could see several large gaps where wooden
planks should have been.

'I'll bet this jetty hasn't been used in years,'
James said, peering from behind Tilly's
shoulder. 'It looks rotted through.'

'Take off your belt, James,' Mandy said.

'What?'

'Take off the belt on your jeans!' Mandy
repeated. 'We'll loop it around Oscar's neck and
pull him out.'

'He'll be strangled,' James said.

'Oh, dear, we've got to do something!' Tilly
said despairingly. Oscar squealed loudly and
thrashed about in the mud. It held him like glue.

'Well, let's give it a try.' James unbuckled his
good leather belt. 'Oh, crumbs,' he said. 'This
is awful.'

'It'll wash,' Tilly said urgently. 'Don't worry.'

'I'm not worried about the belt,' James told
her. 'I'm concerned for Oscar.' Dutifully, James
knelt to remove his trainers, which, even in the

half-light of torch and moon, Mandy could see were coated with slimy ooze. She looked about again for the dog, peering into thickets and even across the water of the lake, but there was no sign of her. She had gone. 'The dog seems to have vanished,' Mandy said. 'She did us a favour though, didn't she, bringing us to Oscar?'

'Yes, we would never have found him in time if it hadn't been for her,' Tilly said.

'Oscar probably would have suffocated in this icky stuff by the morning,' James said, holding his nose. 'Struggling to get out would weaken him and eventually he'd have collapsed.'

'Oh, don't, James, please,' Tilly said. 'Let's go! Coming, Mandy?' Mandy slipped off her shoes. She was grateful that the night was not chilly. Nevertheless, the first contact of mud on her bare feet was a shock, and Mandy gasped at its cool, clinging touch.

'Oh, yuck!' said James in disgust. 'This is gross.'

They waded in, the mud closing around their ankles and calves. It was like walking through chocolate blancmange pudding, Mandy thought, though rather more smelly. But she was so relieved that they had found Oscar that she didn't mind a bit. The pig's little eyes

swivelled frantically in his head at their
approach but he kept still, breathing hard from
his efforts at escape. James slipped his belt
round Oscar's thick neck, then looped the end
through the buckle and tightened his grip.
Oscar grunted loudly in surprise.

'Right,' said Tilly. 'Well done, James. Let's all
pull together.' Six hands found a length of belt
to grasp and tug. Oscar gave a mighty snort, as
he was dragged over on to his side and the foul
mud flowed over and around his cheek and ear.

'Oh no!' cried Tilly. 'All we're doing is getting
him in deeper!'

James plunged his hands into the mud and lifted Oscar's head out of the mud. It came out with a plop that sent mud flying across James's face.

Mandy removed his glasses and cleaned away a splash covering one lens with her sleeve. She replaced them. 'Thanks,' James said gratefully. 'Look, this is no good. We'll have to get help.'

'Yes, I suppose you're right,' Tilly said, looking sadly down at her pig. Oscar, exhausted, was slumped miserably, panting hoarsely. 'Wake Jack, not Gramps, will you?'

'And Mum and Dad too,' Mandy said.

'Me?' James asked.

'Please, James,' Tilly pleaded. 'I want to stay here with Oscar and I'd like Mandy with me. Do you mind?' James shook his head.

'You know where the kitchen is?' Tilly asked him. 'Jack's is the room right next to it. You'll find it. We'll stay here and watch Ozzie. Go as quickly as you can, will you?' Tilly's voice was desperate.

James picked his way slowly out of the mud. As he moved away, the welcome torch light faded and Mandy felt a chill creep down her spine. *Please*, she pleaded silently, *let the moon stay with us until he returns!*

* * *

It seemed to Mandy that hours had passed before she heard the distant, welcome voices of Jack Stone and James and her mum and dad. She and Tilly had huddled together on the shore, a metre away from the mud where Oscar was stuck like a beached whale, their arms round each other for comfort and warmth, their feet crusted over with drying black silt. She and Tilly had been too keyed up to sleep. They had kept a watchful eye on Oscar, in case he sank like a stone. The moon had stayed with them, casting a rippling glow across the far-off water of the lake, lapping just out of Oscar's reach. 'If this was a lagoon,' Mandy had said, 'then the tide would have come in by now and we could've floated Oscar out of trouble!'

'No such luck,' Tilly had said, hugging Mandy closer.

'Hey, I think someone's coming at last!' Mandy had exclaimed a few moments later.

The two girls got shakily to their feet. 'James!' Mandy shouted. 'Over here.' Mr Hope was first to come crashing across the scrubland and on to the shore. He was closely followed by Jack Stone. James jogged along behind with Emily Hope.

'Are you all right, love?' Mrs Hope hugged Mandy and handed her and Tilly a second jumper each. 'Thanks. I'm fine. But poor Oscar, Mum, he's exhausted and so frightened!'

'Thank heavens you found him. Wretched little pig!' Jack said heatedly. He levelled the torch and the beam picked out the lumpish, black shape of Oscar. Mandy, shivering like a jelly, thought he looked like a discarded barrel.

'Oh, Jack,' Tilly said. 'I was so scared that he'd drown. He must have fallen through the wooden slats of that boat jetty.'

'We'll get him out,' Mr Hope said. He had a spade in his hand.

'Well done, James,' Mandy said, giving her friend a thump on the back. 'You've been great.'

'Yes,' Tilly said. 'Thanks.'

James was breathing hard from his dash back to the castle. His arms were covered with a lattice-work of tiny scratches. Mud from the lake had dried on his legs and down one side of his face. 'Poor James,' Mandy mumbled sympathetically.

Jack and Mr Hope had plunged into the mud. Jack held his spade above his head. James followed them in, his face screwed up against the cold and the smell. Jack began shovelling the mud away from Oscar, filling the spade and heaving it aside, while Mr Hope held fast to the rope collar he had slipped round the pig's neck. Oscar squealed in terror, certain he was about to be finished off. The tops of his legs became visible, then the hoof of one stumpy foot. Mr Hope busied himself round his hindlegs and, within minutes, Oscar was free.

'Hooray! Hooray!' chanted Tilly, as Oscar was lugged to the shore by Jack, whose legs were buckling under his enormous weight. 'I can't hold him; he's too heavy,' he said, putting the pig down.

Mrs Hope, waiting at the shoreline of the mud, stepped forward and slipped the rope from round Oscar's neck. She passed it under his muddy tummy, tying it efficiently into a harness of sorts. 'Lead him along on that,' she told Jack. 'It won't strangle him, then.' She stooped to examine Oscar, who was limp with exhaustion. Mrs Hope ran her fingers up and down Oscar's legs, scraping the cloying mud away with her fingernails. After a minute, she stood up.

'I'm afraid he did more than just get stuck in the mud,' Emily Hope said gravely. 'He's got a nasty gash down the side of this back leg. It'll need stitching.'

'Oh, poor Ozzie,' Mandy said. She looked at James. From his pale, tired face, she guessed he'd had enough excitement for one night.

Tilly scratched Oscar's head. 'Don't worry, Ozzie. We're going to take you home and make you better.'

'Let's head over to the yard now, then,' Mr Hope suggested. 'I'm going to need your help in getting Oscar there, Jack. We don't want him to put any pressure on that leg, if we can help it.'

'You go on ahead and get yourselves cleaned up, then rouse Mrs Booth and ask her to make a pot of coffee for us, will you? I hate to wake her, but we need to attend to Oscar immediately and I feel I need something to keep me going,' Mrs Hope said, looking at Mandy, James and Tilly.

'Yes,' said Tilly brightly, as though it were about nine o'clock in the morning and she had just got out of bed. She rolled down the legs of her filthy jeans and started out for the castle.

Mandy and James followed Tilly, who still had a spring in her step, at a more leisurely pace. Mandy felt as though she was sleepwalking, but she was very relieved. Oscar was safe. Her mum and dad would have him back to normal in no time.

'Oi! Just a minute, you lot,' Jack called after them. 'I forgot to ask you . . . just how *did* you come to find Oscar out in the lake in the middle of the night?'

Six

Lights went on all over the castle as Booth and Mrs Booth were woken with the news of Oscar's rescue. Ellie Booth thought better of waking Max Blaithwaite, preferring to surprise him with the good news of Oscar's rescue in the morning. 'He needs his rest,' she reasoned, filling a couple of flasks with boiling water, 'and there isn't anything practical he can do at this hour, except worry.'

Mr Blaithwaite slept on, as Tilly, Mandy and James took turns in the bathroom and hurried into fresh clothing. 'He uses earplugs,' Tilly confided to Mandy, who was scrubbing at her legs with a sponge. 'The whole castle could crumble to the ground and Gramps wouldn't know a thing until he was hit by a falling brick.'

'I'm very glad you've had a wash,' Booth observed, looking at James, Tilly and Mandy's legs. 'I thought I'd been woken by the Loch Ness monster when I first saw you standing at the door of our room, Tilly. And what an awful stench!'

'So did Blackie,' chuckled James. Blackie's tail thumped against James's legs. He seemed to think that they were about to go for a walk. A walk was always welcome, even if it was in the middle of the night.

'Wonderful news, wonderful news,' chanted Mrs Booth, as she bustled about pouring sugar into a small airtight container. 'I'm so delighted Oscar's safe . . . silly old pig that he is.'

'We'll take the car and drive round to the yard,' Mr Booth said decisively. 'I expect you've had enough walking for one night. Coming, Ellie?'

'I'm ready,' she replied, stuffing a packet of biscuits under her arm.

'Sorry, Blackie,' James said, ruffling his dog's fur, 'but I'm bushed.'

They found Mr and Mrs Hope, with Jack,

clustered around Oscar, who was lying in a small pen, in deep straw, on his good side. Mr Hope had cleaned most of the mud off him, and made him as comfortable as possible, but the gaping wound on his leg was open and bleeding. 'Oh, my poor Ozzie,' Tilly said, covering her eyes. The Booths greeted Jack, who was sitting beside Oscar, stroking his ear.

'We really need a second torch,' Adam Hope said. Booth stepped forward and directed a powerful beam of light on to Oscar's wound.

'Thanks,' said Mr Hope, opening his black vet's bag.

'Ugh,' said James. 'That looks really nasty.'

'Oscar, boy, don't worry,' Mandy called softly. 'We're here to make you feel better.' She pushed gently at Blackie, whose nose was working furiously, straining forward to absorb the smell of this strange, grunting creature lying on the ground.

'Yes, it's as Emily thought out at the lake. We'll need to stitch that up,' said Mr Hope, probing gently at the wound.

'But . . . won't it hurt him?' Tilly said, in a small voice.

'I'll give him a local anaesthetic so he doesn't feel a thing, and also a shot of sedative so he doesn't decide to go exploring again halfway through my handiwork!' Mr Hope said. He took a bottle out of his bag, filled a syringe with a pink-coloured liquid and injected it into Oscar's thick neck. Oscar lifted his head and grunted, then flopped it back into the straw.

'That will take about ten minutes to work,' Mrs Hope said, stooping to lift one of Oscar's little eyelids and peer into his eye. 'So we have time to get organised.' She handed Mr Hope a plastic bag of fluid.

'Oh, are you going to put him on a drip?' James asked.

'No. This is a drip bag, you're quite right, James, but I'm just going to use this sterile fluid to wash the mud out of his wound.'

Oscar was now lying peacefully, breathing deeply and evenly. Mr Hope filled a second syringe and injected it into the skin around the deep cut. Then he cleaned his hands carefully with a pack of sterile wipes and eased on a pair of tight, plastic gloves. Meanwhile, Emily Hope used the bag of sterile fluid to flush away the mud, using the syringe to squirt the liquid just where it was needed.

'Let's have the torchlight over here, please, Booth.' The beam was directed on to a rolled-up cloth of shiny silver instruments, and from it Mr Hope selected a scalpel.

'Ooh,' said Tilly. 'I can't watch.' Mandy put an arm round her shoulders.

'I'm only going to neaten up this rather jagged wound, Tilly,' said Mr Hope. 'Then we'll stitch it up and he'll be as good as new.'

'I'll prepare an antibiotic injection,' said Mrs Hope. Mandy saw that Tilly was looking away from where her father worked on Oscar. She was gazing out at the night sky.

'Look,' Mandy said, 'it's starting to get light.' There was a rim of faint orange light on the horizon. James yawned.

'I'm exhausted,' he said.

'Tea, Mrs Hope?' said Mrs Booth, offering a mug.

'Oh, that's welcome, thank you,' she replied.

Mandy accepted a mug and went to stand beside her mother. She badly wanted to tell her about the beautiful dog they had found, who had led them to Oscar and saved his life by doing so, but she didn't want to let Tilly down. Tilly wanted the dog to be their secret. She decided to say nothing.

'You still haven't told me how you came to find Oscar,' Jack said suddenly.

'Tomorrow,' Tilly said quickly. 'It's far too late for any more talking.'

'Early,' said James. 'It's too early, you mean.' And he yawned again.

'You three go to bed now,' Jack suggested. 'You've done a fine night's work. You've saved Oscar's life, that's for certain. I'll let Mr B know the happy news as soon as he wakes up.'

'Thanks, Jack. And thank you, Mr and Mrs Hope,' said Tilly. She linked arms with Mandy and James. 'Come on, team,' she grinned.

James whistled and Blackie's ears pricked up. He took a final, quivering sniff at Oscar, then scampered after them.

When Mandy woke up, the sky she could see through her bedroom window was the same pale and hazy orange it had been when she had fallen asleep. She looked at her watch, puzzled. It read 6 p.m. Sunday evening! She had lost a whole, precious day at the castle while in a deep, dreamless sleep. She dressed quickly and sped down the stairs two at a time.

In the kitchen, Tilly, James, Max Blaithwaite and her parents sat around the large oak table. Booth was making up a fire in the cooking range, while his wife chopped up vegetables for supper. Blackie sat looking up at her with large, shining brown eyes.

'Wow,' said Mandy, 'I've been asleep as for hours. Sorry.'

'We've all had our share,' Mrs Hope laughed.

'Mandy, my dear,' said Mr Blaithwaite, who had half-risen to his feet when Mandy came in. 'Your parents and Tilly have been filling me in on the details of Oscar's rescue. All of you were very brave indeed. Well done.'

'How is he?' Mandy asked, sitting down.

'Fine,' said Mr Hope. 'Jack has proved himself a saintly nurse and reports that Oscar is up and about already, looking for a way out.'

'No chance of that,' Tilly put in. 'Jack's covered every possible escape route.'

'Tilly has been telling us, too, about your ramblings after dark,' Adam Hope began, 'and she . . .'

'I said how we couldn't *wait* to explore – to have an adventure out in the grounds. Which, of course, we did.' Tilly widened her eyes at Mandy and put a discreet finger to her lips. James was studying his fingernail. Mandy didn't know what to say, so she smiled and nodded. It wasn't exactly a lie, she thought. They certainly had had an adventure!

'Well,' Emily Hope said, taking a basket of bread rolls from Ellie Booth, 'now that you have had your little adventure, there will be no further need to leave the castle at night, will there?'

Mandy, James and Tilly looked at each other. 'Probably not,' agreed Tilly. 'When's supper, Mrs Booth? I'm starving.'

They sat up late playing cards in Mandy's room. Blackie, who had spent a busy day down in the yard with Jack Stone while James had been sleeping, now snored gently at the foot of the bed. Mandy was wide awake and even James looked alert and fully recovered. 'I hope,' said Mandy, 'that she comes back. I mean, it would be such a shame if we never saw her again.'

'Who?' asked James absently, shuffling his hand of cards.

'The Aminta dog. She was amazing,' Tilly agreed. 'I just wish I knew where on earth she came from and how she managed to find her way into that dungeon.'

'The way she led us to Oscar ... it was ... creepy,' James said, with a small shudder.

'Do you have to leave tomorrow?' Tilly asked suddenly. 'Wouldn't Mr and Mrs Hope let you stay on a bit longer, so we can solve the mystery together?'

'We could ask . . .' Mandy said, her eyes shining. 'It would be brilliant to stay. I'd hate to miss out on seeing Aminta again.'

'Me too,' said James. 'Let's ask – after all, it is the school holidays.'

'Let's go back – now!' Tilly said, jumping off the bed and upsetting the pile of cards.

'Back where?' James said, looking alarmed. 'That smelly lake?'

'No! The room where the old books are! Let's go and see what's in them!'

'Yes!' said Mandy excitedly. She couldn't help hoping that the dog would be waiting for them. Blackie lifted his head, alerted by the tone of Mandy's voice. He yawned and struggled into a sitting position, blinking expectantly, then scratched his ear lazily.

Tilly was pulling on a sweater, so James hurriedly scooped up the cards and patted them into a pile. He looked doubtful. 'Stay here, boy,' he told Blackie. 'Go back to sleep. Creeping around down there will only make you nervous again.'

Tilly took the torch and led the way down to the kitchen and along to the staircase leading to the basement. A light shone from under the door of Jack Stone's room and Mandy heard the muffled sound of a radio playing softly. As they tiptoed past, Mandy thought briefly about her mother and father. She wasn't disobeying them, she told herself: she was not, after all, going to be leaving the castle.

At the foot of the stairs, Mandy's heart began ticking like a bomb that was about to go off. Her eyes swept the corners of the basement room in the dim light, hoping for a glimpse of the dog.

'No sign of Aminta,' said Tilly.

'Well, she's probably wandered back to her home by now and is curled up by her owner's fire dreaming of being lost in Skelton Castle,' James whispered. Mandy felt a bit disappointed. They crouched and shuffled through the tiny doorway, which was still ajar, and Mandy seized the first of the old books that came to hand. A cloud of dust rose around the heavy old leather binding. Tilly and James crowded round Mandy as she began to turn the yellowed, crisp, parchment pages.

'The writing's difficult to make out,' Mandy said.

'Let me see,' James took the book from Mandy and sat down. 'Point the torch on the page, Tilly.'

James looked closely at the elaborate, curly writing in big black strokes on the pages and began to read: ' "I am the happy owner of three of the noble breed. A fine litter born this day of January 12th, 1770. Two males (Glen and Monarch) destined for the kennels of the Marquis of Hithestowe (as deer trackers) and one bitch, a rough, lightish-grey colour, which I intend to keep here at Skelton Castle, to be named Aminta, from the Greek, meaning 'protector'." '

'Wow,' breathed Mandy. 'Aminta – that name again . . . this is somebody's diary.'

'Probably the first Lord Skelton to have owned and lived in the castle, judging from the date – that's eighteenth century. Gramps told me that's when the first Skeltons came here.'

'Do you think your grandfather knows about these books?' James whispered.

'I'm sure he doesn't.' Tilly said. 'And they might be quite valuable.'

'Listen!' James said, who had turned two pages of the book: ' "I have survived . . ." ' James squinted in the poor light and struggled to make out the strange script, ' "this day the boating accident that took the lives of two men and a leash of my best hounds, among them Cohmstrie, as good a tracker as ever ran, and

Buscar, who was thoroughbred, the best that ever I saw of any kind, save my beloved Aminta, whose courage this day shall not go unrewarded." '

'Read on!' Tilly urged excitedly. 'How did Aminta show courage?'

James mumbled to himself as he skipped over a few lines he couldn't make out. Then, at the bottom of the page, he read: ' "She showed signs of exhaustion after her brave rescue and had swallowed much of the waters of the lake. Fistfuls of her coat remained in my clenched palms long after she had dragged me to the safety of the shore, where we lay gasping till Donaldson came upon us at break of dawn." '

'Wow,' Mandy said again, her eyes as round as saucers. 'What an incredible tale. She saved him from drowning.'

'It doesn't add up,' Tilly said, frowning. 'I mean, why are there so *many* graves in the cemetery, all with the name Aminta on them?'

'Yes,' Mandy frowned, 'and all those portraits of the same type of dog in the little gallery . . .'

'Let's try another book,' James suggested. 'We're bound to find out more. There are all sorts of books here, look. This is the Keeper's Log,' he read, 'Cook's Accounts . . . a map, Kennel Keeper's Record . . .'

There was a fizzling sound and a small pop, and the beam of the torch went out, leaving them in complete darkness.

'Oh, no,' Mandy said, in a very small voice. 'The battery's gone.'

'Crikey,' said Tilly. 'Now it really *does* feel spooky in here.'

'Hold on to me, Tilly, and you James,' said Mandy, groping around to feel for her friends. They made contact, clung for a moment, then began to inch their way in the general direction of the little doorway leading back to the basement room. James struck his head on the wooden chest coming through and cried out loudly.

'Shh!' Tilly cautioned. 'We don't want to wake Jack.'

'Tilly,' Mandy said, as she gratefully reached the bottom of the stone staircase leading up and into the castle, 'we're going to have to tell your grandfather about our discovery in the dungeon. About the books and the dog . . .'

'She deserves to have a name,' James said. 'If we ever see her again, we'll call her Aminta, OK?'

Tilly and Mandy nodded. 'Aminta,' they said together and then climbed the stairs to their rooms in silence.

Seven

Max Blaithwaite was stacking books from a packing crate on to shelves in the library when Mandy, James and Tilly found him the following morning. Booth, who had carried up his breakfast on a round silver tray, had the job of dipping deep into the box and hauling out the heavy volumes one at a time.

'Aha! A joy to see you all on this beautiful morning. Have you breakfasted?' Mr Blaithwaite beamed a sunny smile and, without waiting for a reply, went on: 'Your parents depart for their Ark today, Mandy, and I believe are taking you two away with them, is that so?'

'Gramps,' Tilly said. 'Can they stay? Here, I

mean? For a day or two? Something's come up, you see.'

'Come up?' He looked puzzled.

'We've made an amazing discovery, Mr Blaithwaite. We want to talk to you about it, if you have time,' Mandy said, putting a restraining hand on Blackie, whose curious nose was snuffling in the box.

'All the time in the world, Mandy. And of course you can stay as long as you like at Skelton Castle – with your parents' permission. Booth, another pot of coffee, if you please.'

Booth straightened, with a faint groan, and rubbed his back. 'Certainly, sir. Shall I let the dog out into the grounds?'

'Thanks,' James said. Blackie was being treated royally and was having the time of his life. He wagged his tail when Booth called and trotted after him happily.

'Come and sit down,' Mr Blaithwaite suggested, 'and you can tell me all about it.' He eased himself into a scarlet velvet armchair, facing the huge, gaping mouth of an empty fireplace, smiling with anticipation. Mandy thought how wonderfully cosy the square stone room would be in the winter, with logs ablaze in the grate. She sat on a small oriental rug beside the hearth. James squeezed up beside her, while Tilly paced the polished floorboards.

'Gramps,' she began, 'We've been exploring the castle this weekend . . .' she paused, as though wondering where to begin. Max Blaithwaite had inclined his head and propped his chin in the palm of his hand. He looked so . . . wise – and interested, Mandy thought.

'There's a dungeon, down below the kitchen, and there are some amazing books in it,' Tilly said.

'Records,' James put in.

'The musical variety?' Mr Blaithwaite asked, clearly puzzled.

'No, Gramps, *books*! Old books about Skelton Castle, all sorts of things.'

'There's a diary, written by a Skelton family member, we think, which tells the story of a drowning and about how he was saved by a—'

'A wonderful, big brave dog – a deerhound, like the ones in the picture gallery,' Mandy finished James's sentence. Mr Blaithwaite held up a hand and smiled, his eyes closed.

'Stop!' he ordered. 'My poor head is spinning. You must take me to this Aladdin's cave of treasure at once, so I may see for myself just what it is you have discovered. It could be of significant historical value.'

Just then the heavy oak door to the library was opened by Booth, bearing a silver coffee pot on a tray and several chinking cups and saucers. Behind him were Mr and Mrs Hope. Mandy thought how sad it would be if she never got the chance to see Aminta again and hoped her parents would allow them to stay on for a few more days.

'Mmm, is that coffee I can smell?' Mrs Hope asked.

'Come in, help yourselves. Have you had breakfast?' said Max Blaithwaite.

'We've had the usual Mrs Booth feast, thank you!' Mrs Hope laughed.

'I'm so grateful to you both,' Max Blaithwaite said. 'It's been marvellous having you around to oversee the settling in process. And, of course, to help with Oscar.'

'Ask them, will you, Gramps?' Tilly urged her grandfather in a low voice.

'Eh? Oh, yes. Tilly wondered if it would be all right for Mandy and James to stay on a bit longer . . . marvellous company for Tilly . . . plenty of room, as you know!' Adam and Emily Hope looked at each other for a few seconds.

'No more getting bogged down in muddy

lakes at midnight?' Mrs Hope asked, looking at Mandy.

'I promise,' said Mandy, grinning.

'We'll be back here ourselves in a couple of days,' Mr Hope said, dropping a lump of sugar into his cup. 'To check on Oscar's leg. So we can pick you two up then. If you're sure, Max?'

'Absolutely,' Mr Blaithwaite confirmed. 'How splendid, that's settled then. And will you two be staying to lunch?'

'No, thank you,' Mrs Hope smiled. 'We'll start our journey after coffee, I expect. It's been a marvellous weekend.'

Mandy and Tilly could hardly contain their impatience while the farewells were being said. Booth took an age loading the weekend bags into the Land-rover. Then Blackie jumped into the car and stubbornly refused to get out again, convinced that James was going to drive away without him.

'Go indoors,' prompted Ellie Booth, chuckling. 'That way he'll know you'll be staying on with us.' James went into the kitchen and Blackie, looking very alarmed, leaped out of the car and followed him at a trot. When at last the Land-rover pulled away down the long drive, Max Blaithwaite stopped waving and immediately turned to Tilly. 'Right, now. Lead on! Take me to your dungeon.'

'Oh, Gramps, good for you!' cried Tilly. 'I'll go and get my torch.'

'Needs new batteries!' James yelled, as she sprinted away.

'I know!' Tilly yelled back.

It took Max Blaithwaite some time to negotiate the stone steps leading into the basement room. Mandy was certain that when he saw the tiny doorway to the dungeon he would refuse to go through it. Instead, he muttered: 'Good Lord, are you sure?' and at James's vigorous nodding, he managed to slide through by shuffling backwards on his bottom.

'Torch,' shouted Mr Blaithwaite, when he reached the other side and found himself in pitch darkness.

'Coming through,' Mandy called, slipping through the tunnel-like opening with ease.

'I've got your cane, Gramps,' Tilly said, following. James appeared soon after, with Blackie at his side. Tilly shone her rejuvenated torch on the shelves against the wall. They stood in triumphant silence. Max Blaithwaite let out a long, low whistle of pure amazement.

'Good Lord! What a find. Why, we may never have discovered this dungeon if you hadn't moved that chest aside. I expect it has a gory past . . . if only walls could speak.'

'I'm glad they can't,' Mandy whispered, imagining she could see blood dripping on to the stone floor from the manacles attached to the wall. Max Blaithwaite limped over to the pile of leather-bound, cobweb-strewn books, stacked precariously on the ancient shelves.

'Well, well, well, what an astounding find,' said Mr Blaithwaite again, exhaling a huge puff of air in astonishment. 'Tilly, my dear, just *how* did you discover this place?' He coughed and blinked, looking around in amazement.

'There was this eerie howling, on Saturday night. We thought it might be a wolf. We followed the noise to this room and found . . .'

'A deerhound in the room next door,' Mandy finished. 'She was beautiful. She wouldn't let us touch her but she wanted to get in here – she made that clear enough.'

'A stray? Locked in? Here?' Max Blaithwaite asked, horrified.

'We're not exactly sure,' James said. 'She led us out, though – through that archway there, and down a long underground tunnel, into the cemetery and on down to the lake where Oscar was trapped.'

'But this is all absolutely extraordinary,' said Mr Blaithwaite, clearly dumbfounded by the secrets harboured by his castle. 'The dog must have found her way in through the tunnel, surely? She was after the smell of food wafting down from the kitchen, no doubt.'

There was the sound of knee joints cracking as Max Blaithwaite bent down to take up the first volume to hand. Mandy, James and Tilly fell silent while he began carefully to turn the crisp parchment pages. Mandy saw that his bushy eyebrows had been drawn together in a frown of amazed concentration.

'*Aminta*,' Mandy pleaded to herself, looking into the darkened corners of the cold and fusty-smelling room, '*please come back*.'

'Aminta,' said Mr Blaithwaite, keeping his eyes on the book, 'is the dog that saved Hector Skelton's life. This is a diary of some kind, written by the man himself. It says here that she was buried in the castle graveyard in 1732 . . . She was twelve years old.'

'That's the date we saw carved on one of the gravestones!' James said, excitedly.

'Not the one with the fresh flowers on it?' Tilly asked, open-mouthed.

'No, that one had a more recent date on it,' Mandy said. 'Remember?'

'Keep the torch still, Tilly dear,' her grandfather urged. 'Let me read. It says . . . um . . . let me see . . .' Max Blaithwaite began to read. ' "Nothing could exceed the courage displayed by my Aminta on that day, having struggled through the waters in a most determined way; and whose selfless actions have saved my life. I hereby decree that all future owners of this great castle of Skelton must keep on the land one or more of the breed, seeking out those who are long in body and light of foot – a breed held in such high esteem – to protect the castle . . . a talisman of luck throughout the days to come – and to be lain in the ground at their life's passing in the burial site where my beloved Aminta now lies, a sacred and fitting resting place for all of the castle's valiant protectors . . ." '

Blackie whined, making Mandy jump. James stroked his head and he lay down with a heavy sigh. 'Blackie's cold,' James announced. 'He's shivering all over.'

Max Blaithwaite was unravelling a tightly

folded parchment map, hand-drawn in black ink. 'Here, look,' he said. 'There's the cemetery which you told me about – and, of course, the cemetery of which this dear chap Hector writes. It's clearly marked. And yet it's missing from the map given to me by the Land Registry office.'

'Isn't it wonderfully spooky?' Tilly said, thrilled.

'It's more than spooky,' said her grandfather, carefully storing the ancient map away in the protective folds of the book. 'It means that I've got some work to do. I certainly shan't be responsible for allowing this important piece of history to be sold off for modern housing. I shall have it stopped immediately. I'll go to the law-courts if necessary . . .'

'Hooray!' shouted Tilly, leaping up and down.

'I think Blackie wants to get out,' said James in a small voice. 'I don't think he can breathe in here, or something.' Mandy saw that Blackie was panting and beginning to pace up and down. She suddenly felt hopeful – this was exactly the way Blackie had behaved when he had been alerted to Aminta's presence through her howling. She looked about again, but could see no sign of the dog she now automatically thought of as Aminta.

'Shall we take the books upstairs so we can take time to look over them?' Tilly asked.

'No,' Mr Blaithwaite replied. 'We can't risk damaging them. They've been hidden away down here in the dark for so many years; let's leave them. I intend to come back and examine them at my leisure.'

'I'll take Blackie out now,' James said.

'Yes, I feel the need for some air myself. Let us return through that unpleasant little opening in the wall. I want to telephone my solicitor right away,' said Mr Blaithwaite, feeling for his cane.

James, with Blackie, went through first, and Tilly held the torch for her grandfather. Mandy had stooped to a crouching posture when she glanced back over her shoulder a final time to the arched entrance to the tunnel. She gasped. The great dog was sitting quietly in the tunnel mouth, statue-still, looking back at her through eyes gleaming gold in the fading torchlight. Mandy was overjoyed. Her heart began to hammer with excitement.

'Aminta . . .' Mandy said softly. 'Good girl, Aminta.' At this, the dog cocked her head deliberately to one side, listening intently. 'Tilly!

Look!' Mandy said urgently, clutching and pulling at Tilly's T-shirt. Tilly looked back, just in time to see the dog stand and slowly walk back into the tunnel, and disappear.

'Oh, she came back! Gramps, James!' Tilly shouted. 'The dog was here . . . she . . .'

'Shh!' said Mandy. 'You might frighten her.'

'Well, she's gone again now,' Tilly said, and slipped through the doorway after the others. Mandy followed, reluctantly. She couldn't remain alone in the dark, though she badly wanted to follow Aminta down the tunnel.

Upstairs, Max Blaithwaite, breathing heavily

from the effort of his climb up from the basement, limped off to his study to contact his solicitor on the telephone. 'I'll report back!' he called.

Mandy sat down on the landing. She said to the others: 'Aminta came back! She can't be a stray, she just *can't* be. She's here for a reason. Let's go to the gallery and look at the dog portraits, shall we?' Tilly and James nodded eagerly.

'I think I remember the way,' James said, looking at Blackie's wagging tail in relief. He bounded after them as they hurried off up the staircase to the second floor. 'This way,' said James. 'Along here and in . . . here!'

'Oh, well done,' Mandy said, as James's finger on the light switch brought the windowless little gallery to life. They stood clustered at the heavy wooden door, gaping, as a hundred painted eyes gazed back glassily at them from the walls. Mandy looked along the row of portraits until she came to the one of the deerhound with the distinctive white diamond in the middle of her chest.

'There!' cried Mandy. 'There she is – there's our Aminta.' They all looked to where Mandy was pointing. Though they had only seen her at night, by torchlight, Mandy was suddenly convinced that this was the portrait of the dog in the dungeon.

'Look at that white diamond on its chest,' James breathed.

'It's exactly the same,' Tilly said. 'That's the picture of the dog in our dungeon, no doubt about it.'

Eight

'I wish you'd stop meddling with what's passed!' Ellie Booth pleaded. 'There's no sense in it, Tilly – no good will come of you snooping around down there in the dark, digging up buried secrets.'

Sitting at the kitchen table, Tilly sighed as Ellie plunged another supper dish into the steaming water of the washing-up bowl. 'Your poor, dear grandfather,' Ellie Booth muttered on, scrubbing vigorously, 'Lord only knows what this will do to his health.'

Mandy scooped up her empty plate, and James's, and took them across to Mrs Booth at the sink. 'Thanks for a lovely supper,' she said with a smile, watching Blackie licking up the last traces of rice from a bowl that had been put down for him.

'Gramps is fine,' Tilly asserted, scoring patterns gently on the tablecloth with her knife. 'He's just trying to do the right thing. As soon as he can get hold of his solicitor then we can save the burial ground of the castle's dogs . . .'

'Graveyards . . . ghost dogs . . . howling in the dungeon . . . I don't like it, I don't like it one bit!' Mrs Booth said firmly, her cheeks flushed pink from fervour and the heat in the kitchen. Tilly ignored her. Her eyes shone with excitement. She sipped at a glass of juice and said: 'Do you *really* think the dog could be a ghost?'

'Well, it doesn't seem to eat, or drink,' James pondered. 'I mean, there's no supper dish or water bowl around, is there?'

'She,' Mandy corrected, 'She, James, not *it*.'

'She, then,' James said.

'The dog in the painting is her exact replica. I suppose that's possible,' Mandy reasoned. 'Dogs can be alike . . . there may be another living stray dog about that looks just like her.'

'But remember the way she managed to slip through the doorway into the dungeon, the first time we went down – and it was only open a few centimetres!' Tilly said.

'Mm, the way she appears suddenly, then vanishes . . .' Mandy added. 'And won't let us touch her.'

'Enough!' said Ellie Booth, thoroughly perplexed, 'We'll all be having nightmares in our beds. I'm off to mine right now, and you should be too.'

'In a while,' Tilly said. 'We'll put the lights off down here when we go, OK?' Impulsively, Tilly jumped up from the table and gave Mrs Booth a hug. 'Don't *worry*!' Ellie Booth shook her head, frowning.

'I don't like it,' she said again, and left the kitchen to make her way to bed. Tilly sat down. 'Shall we play cards?'

'I don't really feel like it . . .' Mandy began, then sat bolt upright in her chair, her eyes wide.

'Howoooooooo . . .'

They waited for the dying echo of the howl to finish. Then, Mandy slapped her palms down on the table in triumph, making James start. He put out a hand for Blackie, wanting to comfort him. 'There you are,' Mandy said, 'She's come back for us. Shall we get the torch?'

'I'll go!' said Tilly, jumping up.

The howling came again, much louder than they had previously heard it, because now they were directly above the basement room that led to the dungeon. Gooseflesh prickled along Mandy's arms. Blackie began to pace, panting hard.

'Here we go again,' James said, tying his shoelace. 'Who knows where we may end up tonight.' He chuckled. 'Scotland, perhaps?'

'You *want* to go, don't you?' Mandy asked him.

'Yeah, only, I wish she'd come to us in the daytime. Why does it always have to be dark?'

'Yes,' Mandy agreed, 'that's another odd thing about her.'

Aminta howled again as Tilly appeared in the kitchen with the torch. 'Spare batteries,' she puffed, brandishing a packet at James. 'Let's go!'

'I'm going to leave Blackie here, in the kitchen,' James said. 'I don't want him to be frightened.'

'Good idea,' Mandy said, stooping to plant a kiss on Blackie's soft head. 'Don't worry, boy. Go back to sleep – we'll be back soon.'

Mandy dashed to the fridge and snatched up a slice of roast meat left over from supper. 'Hang on, Aminta,' she said to herself. 'We're coming.'

* * *

The arc of the torch picked out Aminta in the shadowy, farthest corner of the basement room, wedged between the right angles of stone wall.

'Hello, girl,' Mandy said softly.

The great dog looked more blue in colour than Mandy remembered. She carried her head high, and her yellow gaze was level and calm. She didn't stand up and wag her tail in greeting, although, Mandy thought, she knew them all now and might have been expected to do so. Her neck was long and arched and her thin, shaggy tail lay still and curled on the floor in the shape of the letter C. Instinctively, Tilly, Mandy and James held back, though Mandy longed to approach her.

'Wait for her to guide us,' Mandy whispered to the others. They waited, huddled in the semi-darkness, and Mandy became aware that Tilly was holding tightly to the leg of her jeans in excitement. Mandy loosened Tilly's grip, crouched, and lobbed the slice of roast meat across the floor. It landed with a little plop at the feet of Aminta.

'What's that?' hissed James.

'Meat,' Mandy answered. 'Let's see if she's

hungry.' But Aminta showed no interest at all in the tasty morsel beneath her nose. She moved neither to investigate its scent nor to eat it. Instead, she stood and stepped delicately, gracefully, along the far wall, so that Tilly had to follow her with the torch. She glided through the small doorway to the dungeon beyond. They looked at each other, then scrambled after her.

'The trail has begun,' James said melo-dramatically, brushing dust off the knees of his jeans. 'I hope that Oscar is safely in his bed tonight!' he chuckled.

'Idiot!' Tilly laughed, very softly. Mandy thought how strange it was that none of them wanted to risk offending Aminta by any brash or noisy behaviour.

'She trusts us,' Mandy said. 'She really trusts us and I'm sure she's trying to tell us something. Are we agreed that we'll follow – wherever she wants us to? I think it's too important *not* to.'

James hesitated for only a second before he nodded. 'Agreed,' he said solemnly, glad that he had left Blackie in the kitchen.

'Agreed,' Tilly repeated. 'Hold this, will you?' She passed the torch to James, who went on ahead.

Aminta stood by the arched doorway, looking back over her shoulder as though silently urging them to follow her down the passage to the graveyard. They hurried over the sloping stone floor of the tunnel, breathing in the smell of damp and centuries past. Mandy felt her way with her feet. She hesitated to put out a hand to the ancient, curved walls, fearful of small creatures buried in the crevices of the rock. 'Ugh,' said James, 'Look at these cobwebs.'

The circle of torchlight was like a halo above Aminta's sleek head as she trotted along purposefully, her claws tapping on the stone floor. When the stale air in the tunnel began to smell fresher, Mandy knew they were near the end and felt relieved. The moon had turned the cloudless sky a midnight blue in colour, and cast a ghostly light over the gravestones in the cemetery. 'Thank heavens for the moon,' said Mandy.

'Look,' said Tilly, 'The white daisies have gone from that grave. Someone's put some different flowers there instead.'

'Honeysuckle,' Mandy observed.

Aminta again paused at the cemetery gate, then slipped ahead, moving like quicksilver, on down through the tangled copse of trees. They hurried after her. Mandy's jeans were snagged by a bramble; Tilly was stung by a nettle. 'Ouch!' she said, but didn't slow down. 'Keep up, James, will you? We don't want her to get away.'

'She'll wait for us,' James said, trying to direct the torch beam so that it was of benefit to all of them at once.

'Look!' Tilly said. 'She's sitting down. Is she having a rest?'

They formed a group, carefully maintaining a good distance between themselves and Aminta. She sat statue-still, looking ahead of her. Then Mandy saw what it was Aminta had brought them to. The vast, hulking body of an earth-moving machine, a mechanical digger, towered above the tallest tree. Its garish yellow body looked horribly out of place among the soft greens and earth colours in the wood. The metal neck of the machine arched and stretched towards the ground, the huge bucket poised to strike, like some ghastly prehistoric monster.

'Oh, no!' James said. 'The machines are already in position for the demolition of the graveyard!'

'I hadn't realised the work would begin so soon,' Tilly gasped. 'This is dreadful.'

'Look,' said Mandy miserably, 'there are white

crosses marked with chalk on these lovely old trees. That probably means they're going to be cut down, too.'

'There's another . . . and another,' Tilly cried. 'Oh, they're going to get rid of them all.' Tilly walked from one doomed tree to another, rubbing with her fingertips at the chalk in an attempt to wipe it away. All she succeeded in doing was smearing it a bit.

Mandy stood staring around her as Tilly and James moved away with the torch. She stood in a pool of pale moonlight, feeling the weight of sorrow inside her like a stone. Aminta sat with her back to Mandy, waiting patiently. 'Aminta!' Mandy called softly. 'Aminta, I'm so sorry for you. They mean to take your graveyard away, girl. But we're going to help you, I promise. We'll do everything we can – and Mr Blaithwaite is going to stop it. He said he would . . .'

Just then James and Tilly came running back. 'They've hacked away all the ivy from the cemetery gate,' James said, flashing the torch in Mandy's face. 'They really mean business.'

'Hey,' said Mandy, 'you're blinding me with that torch.'

'Sorry,' James said. 'Oh, look, Aminta's

leaving again.' Mandy got to her feet and Tilly linked arms with her.

'Don't look so upset,' she said to Mandy resolutely. 'We're going to stop this before it goes any further.'

Aminta was moving ahead, picking her way carefully through the leaves of curly copper beech and around the sturdy bulk of thick oak trunks. They hurried to catch her up.

'We're going a bit too far,' James cautioned, after a further fifteen minutes. 'I don't think your grandfather would be too happy about this.'

'Aminta won't lead us into any danger,' Mandy said, convinced that she was right. 'We'll be all right, James,' she added, although she, too, was beginning to wonder just where they were headed. Aminta appeared to be quite certain of the route she was taking across the vast grounds of Skelton Castle.

'It's getting late,' James said, pausing to peer at his watch. 'It's after ten o'clock – I think we ought to turn back.'

'No,' Tilly said. 'Look, down there – she's stopping.'

Aminta had trotted down the sloping side of a grassy bank and come to a halt at the bottom.

Beyond her, Mandy could see the moonlit outline of a dry-stone wall in need of some repair. A thatched peak of roof with one leaning brick chimney stuck up above it reminded Mandy of a feather on a hat.

'It's that small cottage we saw when we first arrived. We must be near the main gates,' she said in surprise.

'There are a few lodgings marked on Gramps's map,' Tilly confirmed. 'I've seen them. But I didn't know that anybody was *living* in them!' Lights were burning in two of the downstairs windows and through the first, larger window, they could see a woman at a table, sewing. Aminta was sitting directly outside the wooden front door, looking up at a large brass knocker expectantly.

'Is this where Aminta lives, do you think?' James said incredulously.

'Surely . . . she can't have brought us all this way to . . . to meet her owners!' Tilly said.

'No,' Mandy asserted. 'I don't believe that for a minute. I think she wants us to go in.'

'Go in?' James exploded. 'We can't! We don't know them, they don't know us . . . We might frighten them if we knock at night – and what will we say?'

Mandy didn't answer because, at that moment, Aminta lifted her paw and scraped long and hard at the door. Immediately, the woman in the window put down her sewing and stood up, a puzzled frown on her elderly face.

'Now we're for it,' hissed James. 'Let's go!'

'No!' Mandy cried. 'Wait . . . look . . .'

Aminta had vanished. Melted away in the darkness as though they had, after all, imagined her. There was the sound of the key turning in the lock and the door ground open with a protesting creak from an unoiled hinge. Light from the room spilled out into the night.

Nine

An old man stood at the door of the cottage, looking out into the night, an expression of surprise on his face. He glanced up at the moon, then from side to side. 'Is anyone there?' he called in a thin, wavering voice.

Mandy hesitated for a second, then she stepped out boldly from behind a bush on the crest of the hill. James made a grab for her, but she was too quick for him.

'Hello,' Mandy said loudly, wondering if the man would be able to hear her. 'Over here.' She waved. 'I'm sorry to bother you, but . . .' She ran down the hill and stepped through a section of the wall that had crumbled to rubble.

'Do you own a dog – about this high?' She held the side of her hand against her ribcage. 'Shaggy, blue-grey coat . . .?'

'A deerhound?' said the man in a rasping voice. 'There ain't no more of them around here. Not now.' He looked at his wristwatch.

'I'm really sorry.' Tilly smiled, stepping forward. 'We shouldn't have bothered you. I'm Matilda Blaithwaite, from Skelton Castle, up on the hill there.' James had made his way slowly to the front porch of the cottage. Mandy felt as though she had a wild bird trapped in her chest, her heart hammered so fiercely. Yet, to her surprise, the man didn't seem in the least angry at their late-night intrusion.

'I know who you are,' he said. 'You're the granddaughter of the new owner. We wondered when you'd visit, but we didn't expect it to be in the middle of the night!'

'We're sorry,' Mandy repeated.

'Who is it, Tom?' The woman they had seen sewing in the window appeared at his side. She wore a dressing-gown. 'Mercy! It's children. Out at this time of night! Come in, come in!'

'They was looking for a lost dog, Molly. A deerhound,' the man said, standing aside as Tilly, Mandy and James shuffled into the tiny hall.

'I'm Molly Noble and this is my husband, Tom,' said the woman. 'I'll pop the kettle on. I expect you could do with a warm drink. Hot chocolate do you? You've walked quite a distance if you've come from up at the castle.'

Mandy and James looked at Tilly, who shrugged at them and made a face. 'Why not?' she whispered. 'We might find out a bit more about Aminta.'

'It is rather late for us to be visiting, Mr Noble,' Mandy said. 'We can come back another time, if you'd rather.'

'My wife and I are poor sleepers. We generally stay up late, so don't worry about keeping us up. Does your grandfather know you're out and about so late, Miss?' He glared at Tilly.

'Sort of,' Tilly mumbled. Mandy had a sudden vision of Max Blaithwaite asleep in his room at the castle, unaware that his granddaughter and her friends were out roaming the grounds. Yet, Mandy felt certain, somehow, that Mr Blaithwaite would approve.

'Here we are, then,' said Mrs Noble, shuffling in with a heavily laden tray. She set it down on a table in the sitting-room. 'Sit down, please.'

Mandy sank gratefully on to a worn rug and rested her back against a sofa. She hadn't realised until this moment how tired her legs were. James sat cross-legged on the floor and Tilly sank into a big armchair with a heavy sigh. 'Wow, it's good to sit down.'

'We're so glad you came, aren't we, Tom?' Molly Noble smiled warmly at her husband. He nodded.

'Now what's this about a lost deerhound?' he asked.

'We don't know who she belongs to, Mr Noble,' Mandy spoke up. 'She's a gorgeous dog who . . . kind of . . . comes and goes . . .'

'We followed her here, to your cottage. This is where she seemed to want to be. It was the dog who scraped on the door for your attention, not us.' James put in.

'Ah, yes,' said Mr Noble dreamily, looking up at the beamed ceiling. 'Do you know about deerhounds as a breed?' Mandy, James and Tilly shook their heads. Mrs Noble handed them each a mug of hot chocolate.

'Look fierce, but are as gentle as doves on the inside. They're as fast and powerful and fearless a breed as you'll get. The Phoenicians were said to have brought the first deerhounds to these shores as hunting dogs, way back in the year 1000 BC, and, as they moved north, they developed a rough coat, for warmth.' Tom Noble paused to sip his tea. He was clearly enjoying having someone to talk to, Mandy thought. 'Deerhounds were used in Scotland to hunt deer and stags in the Highlands. They were favoured by Highland chieftains. Anyone below the rank of earl was forbidden to own one.'

'Tell them about Aminta, dear,' Molly Noble said, delicately stirring a lump of sugar into her tea. Mandy sat bolt upright; Tilly's mouth dropped open. James swallowed a mouthful of tea too quickly and nearly choked.

'Ah, Aminta,' Tom Noble said and paused, looking sad. 'There's always been a deerhound or two at Skelton Castle, until now, that is. Molly and me, you see, we worked for the last Miss Skelton, who lived in the castle before your grandfather bought it.'

'Miss Amelia Skelton,' Mrs Noble said. 'As kind as could be, she was. I was her housekeeper for years, and Tom was groundsman.'

'Oh,' Tilly said. 'We didn't know that. But we knew Miss Skelton had died.'

'The first Sir Hector Skelton, who owned the castle many years ago,' Tom Noble said, 'was saved from drowning by his faithful deerhound, Aminta. That's the way the story goes, anyway.

You can take it or leave it.' Mandy, James and Tilly exchanged glances. They already knew this part of the story to be fact.

'So he made it a sort of rule, you see, that all the future owners of this castle should have at least one deerhound as a protector. It was kept to faithfully. Generations of Skelton Castle's owners have kept a deerhound, or more, on the property, and in each group there has been one named Aminta, after the brave lass that saved Sir Hector.'

'How wonderful,' Mandy said. 'That explains the graveyard we found.'

'Ah, yes,' Mrs Noble sighed. 'We try to take care of it, from time to time. But with our old bones it isn't easy now.'

'Well,' Tom Noble went on, getting into his stride, 'Miss Amelia Skelton's own Aminta was the light of her life. She loved her, so she did, as the dog loved her mistress. Then, one night, Miss Skelton called Molly and me to her bedside.'

'Ah, it was a shame to see her so upset,' Molly Noble remembered. 'She was the last surviving member of the generations of Skeltons, you see – and she was terribly troubled by the fact that, when they were gone, not only would there be no Skelton to run the castle, but no deerhound to protect it from an uncertain future.'

'She had come up with a plan for making sure that a deerhound survived her to stay on here as protector,' Tom Noble told them. 'So Aminta was sent away for a time, and when she came back she was carrying a litter of pups.'

'How brave she was . . . poor Miss Amelia,' sniffed Mrs Noble, lost in sad memories of Miss Skelton's last days. 'She had clung to life, frail as she was, waiting desperately for the day when Aminta's puppies would be born, so she could die in peace.'

'Did Aminta succeed in time?' Tilly asked, her eyes wide.

'Just one single female pup was born,' Tom Noble said. 'The other little ones were sickly and too weak to survive.'

'She was overjoyed when Tom took the tiny puppy in to her. She held it to her cheek and kissed it. "Aminta," she said to the puppy, "make sure Skelton Castle falls into the right hands when I'm gone." And with that, her mission completed, she closed her eyes and was gone from this world.' Molly Noble wiped her nose with a lace handkerchief.

Mandy's eyes stung with quick tears. 'What a

sad story! I expect the puppy died, too, did it?'
She could hardly bear to hear the answer to
this question.

'No,' Tom Noble said, softly. 'It did not. Miss
Skelton made Molly and me a gift of this
cottage, so that we could live out our days here
in peace. She gave us the puppy, too.'

There was brief silence in the room. 'But . . .'
said Mandy, 'I thought . . .'

'I thought you said the puppy was to be the
future protector of Skelton Castle,' James said,
puzzled.

'Aye, we did, lad. But only if they were the
kind of people who were worthy of carrying on
the tradition, if you get my meaning.'

'Worthy?' Tilly said.

'Miss Skelton made us promise that we would
not hand over little Aminta to just *anybody* who
took over the castle. We were, she said, to wait
until we were certain that Aminta would be
valued and respected by people who loved and
respected the castle too – and its great history,'
Molly Noble said firmly.

'What happened to Aminta – the mother
dog?' Mandy asked. 'She couldn't, by any
chance, have . . . become lost?'

'Lost!' Mrs Noble said. 'Good heavens, no.

She was adored around here. No, Aminta died, soon after her beloved mistress.'

'Oh!' Mandy felt a stirring of sadness mixed with excitement. She asked: 'What did Aminta look like? Did she have any unusual markings?'

'She had a marvellous white diamond in the middle of her chest,' Tom Noble said. 'An unusual mark . . . quite distinctive.'

Tilly gaped at Mandy, who gaped at James. Tilly coughed. 'Are you . . . um . . . sure . . . Aminta is dead?

'She died in my arms,' Molly Noble told her. 'Right here beside the hearth. She was a wonderful mother to her little pup, and fed her dutifully until she was old enough to eat a bit of solid. Then, it was as if the light went out of her. She lost her energy, her will to live . . .'

'Pined away,' Tom Noble put in. 'Dogs do die of broken hearts, you know. She went to be with Miss Skelton. That's where she belonged. At her mistress's side.'

Nobody spoke. Mandy's thoughts were racing. Aminta *had* come to them, she knew it all along. Their Aminta was definitely the same dog that Mr and Mrs Noble had described. There was no longer any doubt in her mind.

'The puppy?' Mandy asked. 'May we see it, please?'

Mr and Mrs Noble looked at each other.

'Well, now,' Tom Noble began uncomfortably. 'That all depends. You see, we've heard terrible things about the graveyard being sold off – about modern houses being put up, with security gates and guards and about the Skelton land being divided for profit.'

'We're very unhappy about it,' Molly Noble said apologetically. 'We don't feel that, with all this going on, the castle is a suitable place for little Aminta.'

'But you don't understand,' cried Tilly, leaping out of the chair. 'My grandfather didn't divide the land to sell it. He only bought the piece that was left to buy. And he's going to have it stopped. He's been trying to get hold of his solicitor to tell him not to allow this demolition to go ahead.'

Molly and Tom Noble looked hard at each other. 'Is this the truth?' Tom Noble asked, frowning.

'Absolutely,' James cried. 'Tilly's grandfather is committed to keeping the cemetery, now that he knows it's there and how historically important it is.'

'Tilly and Mr Blaithwaite have only been in the castle for a few days, said Mandy, 'but in that short time we've learned the importance of saving this cemetery. You must trust us, Mr and Mrs Noble. Please. We're on your side.'

'Your grandfather will get the demolition work stopped?' Mr Noble said. 'The land will never be divided, nor the castle knocked down, nor the grounds ripped up?'

'Cross my heart and hope to die,' Tilly said solemnly.

'No security fencing?' Molly Noble said.

'Not a metre of it, anywhere.' Tilly said.

Molly Noble smiled with relief. 'Well, in that case,' she said, 'I'll go and wake Aminta – just for you to see, mind. Agreed, Tom, dear?'

'Aye, Molly, love,' Tom Noble said. 'You do that.'

Ten

Aminta was carried into the sitting-room in Molly Noble's arms. She blinked, brown eyes hazy from sleep, and looked around in bewilderment at the collection of faces looking back at her. 'Oh,' Mandy said, 'she's absolutely gorgeous.' Set down on the carpet, the puppy's long, slender legs wobbled and she sat down abruptly, then yawned and tumbled on to her side, legs wiggling comically.

James laughed. 'How old is she?'

'She's about two and a half months old now,' Tom Noble told him. 'She's been a good girl, too, since she lost her mum. She's quick to learn.'

Aminta stood up and bounded over to have a closer look at the visitors. She put her front paws on Tilly's knees and stretched up with her nose to smell her face. Mandy noticed that she had the same white diamond shape on her small chest. Her coat was darker, sleeker, and her tail was smooth rather than shaggy, but it was her adorable little face that stole Mandy's heart. Tilly gathered Aminta into her lap and planted a kiss on the top of her head and Mandy went over to fondle her silky ears, raised up high in excitement and folded over at the top, like an envelope.

'She's so cute!' Tilly said. 'But how would you both feel about Aminta coming to live at the castle?'

'It's her rightful place,' Tom Noble said gruffly. 'We'll miss her, but that's the job she was bred for and that's where she's meant to be.'

'You'll be welcome to visit any time,' Tilly assured them.

Molly Noble suddenly looked at her watch. 'You'd better be getting back now, all of you. It's so late! Tom and I will contact your grandfather tomorrow with our decision. Will that be all right?' She scooped Aminta into her arms.

Mandy struggled to mask her disappointment, and saw that Tilly was, too. She should have realised that there was no way they were going to be allowed to take little Aminta away with them tonight. It would be too unsettling for the puppy, and Mr and Mrs Noble still seemed to need convincing that Max Blaithwaite's intentions for Skelton Castle were truly honourable.

Aminta strained in Molly Noble's arms, cocked her head and yapped as Tilly, Mandy and James left the cottage. Mr and Mrs Noble stood and waved to them in the doorway, having insisted that James replace the batteries in the torch before they left.

'If you see that stray deerhound again,' Tom Noble called, 'let me know, will you?'

'We will,' Tilly called, and nudged Mandy hard with her elbow. 'Bye.'

'Come in!' shouted Max Blaithwaite, as Tilly banged on the door with her fist the following morning. 'Jupiter, child, you'll have the door down – and it's probably one that centuries of marauding armies failed to conquer.'

'Gramps!' said Tilly. 'We've got to talk to you!' Tilly was still in her pyjamas, having shaken a

sleepy Mandy and James awake soon after eight
o'clock. She hurried over to the desk behind
which her grandfather was sitting, poring over
a sheaf of important-looking documents. Mandy
and James hesitated at the door. 'Come along
in, my dears,' Mr Blaithwaite invited them.
'Don't mind the mess. I'm getting straightened
out. Well, Tilly, what have you discovered this
time?'

'Gramps,' she began again, 'you and I have a
duty to make sure that this castle of ours has an
Aminta – without delay!'

'An Aminta!' said Mr Blaithwaite, wrinkling
up his nose in complete confusion. 'What *can*
you mean, my dear girl?'

'Remember Sir Hector Skelton's diaries?'
Mandy prompted eagerly. 'The deerhound that
saved him from death . . . the graveyard he set
up in her honour . . . and his wish that all future
owners of the castle continue the tradition of
owning a deerhound as protector?'

'Ah, yes, yes. There's no need to concern
yourselves about that now. I've been in touch
with Nigel Holden, my solicitor, who has in
turn been in touch with Peter Weeks, the
property developer. In principle, the man is
prepared to accept the sum of money I've

offered him in return for the land.'

'Oh, well done Gramps! That's terrific news. But . . .'

'I had the devil's own job of getting hold of Nigel Holden, who struggled to track down Mr Weeks,' Mr Blaithwaite went on. 'Seems Nigel had been holidaying abroad. But, late last night, when you were all sound asleep in your beds, the call we were hoping for came through from Mr Weeks. Charming man . . . most obliging.' He chuckled in a satisfied sort of way.

'Mr Blaithwaite,' Mandy said, 'Tilly and James and I have been following a trail of clues since Saturday night and the clues have led us to the most wonderful deerhound puppy – called Aminta – who belongs here, as the castle's protector!'

'Can we keep her, please?' Tilly pleaded, her elbows on her grandfather's desk, her face centimetres from his. She gabbled off the details of the previous night's adventure. Eventually she drew breath.

'Well, I've never been against having another dog, as you know, Tilly,' Mr Blaithwaite said, holding Tilly at bay with the flat of his palm. 'Now that we have the room for one, I don't see why not. Dogs need plenty of space, I believe, and regular walking.' Mr Blaithwaite suddenly looked thoughtful. 'Well, I must say, this is all very confusing. I think that what you are trying to tell me is that you believe the ghost of this pup's mother led you to her – is that it?'

'Yes,' Tilly said, triumphantly. 'That's exactly what happened. Aminta – the mother dog – also showed us that the diggers are already in place for destroying the graveyard of her ancestors!'

'Well, they won't get any farther than where they are now. And I, for one,' smiled Max Blaithwaite, 'am certainly grateful to this mysterious Aminta for the part she played in rescuing poor Oscar. A marvellous animal, indeed.'

Tilly slung an arm round her grandfather's shoulder. 'Thanks, Gramps,' she said. 'Thanks for believing . . .'

'Thanks for taking action!' James said.

'I'm sure Aminta will rest in peace, knowing that the graveyard is safe and that her puppy is here at Skelton Castle. You could call the puppy Minty, for short,' Mandy suggested.

'Yes,' said Tilly happily. 'Minty – perfect!'

'Supposing Mr and Mrs Noble decide not to let you have her, after all?' James said gloomily.

'They have to!' Tilly said. 'We're suitable, after all. Anyone can see that.'

The old-fashioned telephone on Max Blaithwaite's desk trilled loudly, making them all jump. Mr Blaithwaite made a grab for it. Tilly seized Mandy round the waist and danced her about excitedly. 'I'm going to have a puppy! I'm going to have a puppy!' she chanted. James grinned at them. Then they heard Mr Blaithwaite say:

'Good heavens! Really? Oh, it can't be so! Yes, of course, I'll do my best. Thank you.'

'What?' Tilly and Mandy said together, when Mr Blaithwaite had put down the telephone.

'Tilly, Mandy, James, you must go quickly to the site of this cemetery. At once! Mr Weeks telephoned from London. He is perfectly willing to call a halt to his digging, but has failed to contact his contractor – the man who is due to dig up the site. I had no idea it was to begin so soon.' Mr Blaithwaite wrung his hands.

'When?' Mandy whispered, horrified.

'This very morning. They might have started already.' Tilly sprang for the door, shouting for James and Mandy to follow. 'I'll get Booth to help me down there as soon as possible – entreat the man to wait, for heaven's sake . . .'

But they didn't hear the end of Mr Blaithwaite's sentence. Tilly was streaking through the corridors of the castle, her feet slapping loudly on the stone floors. Mandy and James charged after her. *Don't let it be too late, please*, Mandy pleaded silently. *We can't let you down now, Aminta, we just can't!*

Tilly chose the route through the gardens of the castle, and Mandy guessed she would have dismissed the idea of taking the tunnel because she hadn't had time to collect her torch. James soon overtook Tilly and went racing ahead towards their goal. Mandy followed, as fast as she could, but found it difficult to see clearly because her eyes kept filling with nervous tears.

'Hey!' yelled James, as he saw the mighty stones of the ancient cemetery wall up ahead. 'Wait! Stop!' The ominous sound of the deep rumbling of a powerful engine could clearly be heard. Hearing James shout, Mandy angrily swiped at the tears and used every last bit of her energy to go faster. She was in time to see James fling himself round the corner of the wall, his sides heaving with his effort, then stumble and fall on his knees. Tilly was seconds behind James. The digger, they saw, had been driven up to the gate of the graveyard.

They stood and gaped, panting. The engine had been started, but there was no sign of the driver – in or out of the machine. They looked around. 'Nobody here,' James gasped.

'Someone must be about. The machine's going . . .' Mandy gasped.

'Oi! Is somebody out there?' The furious shout came from within the cemetery itself. James, Tilly and Mandy hurried along the wall to the gate where the ivy had been hacked away. Although they had left the gate open when they had come through the previous evening, it was now closed, though not padlocked. Behind the black, wrought-iron bars of the gate, the red and perspiring face of a stocky, angry man could be seen. He peered through the bars, his fists clenched by his side.

'Meddling kids!' he spat. 'You call off your dog, d'you hear me? I've been held a prisoner in here for an hour or more. Get the brute locked up so I can get on with my work!'

'Dog?' said Tilly, looking up and down the outer wall of the graveyard.

'We don't have a dog . . . except Blackie, and he's in the kitchen with Mrs Booth having his breakfast,' Mandy said, her heart pumping with joy. *Good old Aminta*, she cheered silently.

'Are you sure,' James said mischievously, 'that you didn't just *imagine* a dog?'

'I've got work to do!' screamed the man. 'That dog has been snarling at me through this gate, I tell you. I switched on my excavator, then came in here to look around and the beast wouldn't let me out again! Waste of good diesel. My mobile phone's been ringing its head off in the cab, and I've not been able to get out to answer it!'

Tilly, Mandy and James grinned happily at each other.

'It's just as well,' Tilly said. 'Because the work here has been cancelled – by Mr Weeks, your boss in London.'

'What?' The man snatched his cap off his head and flung it to the ground in irritation.

'That's what we came to tell you,' Mandy said sweetly. 'Mr Weeks is not having the site cleared any more, thank you.'

'Stand aside,' he bellowed. Tilly opened the gate and they made way for him to pass. The man put one foot outside the gate, and looked warily up and down for the sign of a dog. 'Big, hairy, grey thing, it was, teeth bared,' he mumbled, 'like something out of a horror film.' He picked up his cap.

'Hello!'

The man, who was wiping his forehead with his cap, turned. Max Blaithwaite was limping along towards them, Booth holding his arm. 'My dear fellow! What a lot of inconvenience we've put you to. It's all changed, you see. We're keeping the land intact. Glad we caught you in time. I'm Max Blaithwaite, castle owner.' He put out his hand.

'I won't bother, thank you, sir. I've had a bad

start to the day and I'll just take my excavator now and leave, if you don't mind. You want to lock up that brutish dog of yours, sir, if you don't mind my saying.'

Max Blaithwaite's hand fell limply to his side. He frowned in bewilderment as the man climbed into the excavator. 'Dog?' he said, 'What dog?'

Mandy, Tilly and James burst out laughing. It was with a sense of real triumph that they watched the excavator being driven away.

'Well,' said Mr Blaithwaite. 'There is no accounting for the manners of some people, eh, Booth? A nice pot of tea is what we all—'

He was interrupted by the sound of excited yapping. A soft grey bundle of fur on very long legs was loping towards them across the grass. Her ears flew behind her and her pink tongue lolled.

'Minty!' shouted Mandy in delight.

'Minty!' cried James and Tilly. The puppy bounced and jumped about in an ecstasy of excitement, trying to lick the many hands that reached out to her simultaneously.

'Gramps,' said Tilly, 'This is Minty, the puppy we were telling you about.'

'She's wonderful! But will she get along with

Oscar?' Max Blaithwaite said wearily.

Tom and Molly Noble were standing shyly a few metres away. In Molly's hand was a bunch of pale pink rosebuds. Tom spoke up, 'She's a good girl, sir,' he said. 'She'll do as she's told.'

'Can we keep her then? Mr and Mrs Noble? Gramps?' Tilly burst out with enthusiasm.

'She'd be very welcome, Tilly,' said Max Blaithwaite.

'We saw the digger driving away,' said Molly Noble happily. 'We're so relieved. And of course you can keep her.'

When Mrs Noble had left her roses on Aminta's grave, she and her husband were persuaded to come back to the castle with Minty to settle her in. They walked slowly, keeping to Max Blaithwaite's gentle pace, enjoying the sight of Minty tumbling through the undergrowth. The garden, Mandy thought, was going to be a perfect playground for little Minty.

They came across Mr and Mrs Hope, trudging back up the hill from the yard with Jack Stone. Blackie was with them. Seeing the bigger dog, Minty lay down on her tummy and rolled over on to her back, allowing Blackie to sniff her all over. Blackie's tail pounded a welcome, and Minty got up again to play. 'Mum!

Dad!' Mandy shouted and ran to them. 'We've had the most brilliant time.'

'Hello, everyone,' said Adam Hope cheerfully. 'Goodness, Mandy, you look at if you haven't been to sleep since last we saw you!'

'I'm sorry we weren't around to welcome you back,' Mr Blaithwaite said. 'We were forced to dash away to solve a problem we had . . .'

'Don't worry about that. We know our way round. We went to see Oscar, who's looking much happier,' Emily Hope laughed. 'But, who is *this*?' Minty put her front paws on Emily Hope's knees and wagged her tail. 'You've acquired a puppy in the couple of days we've been away?'

'This is Minty – and it's a long story!' Tilly laughed.

Mr Blaithwaite introduced Mr and Mrs Noble to the Hopes and Jack Stone. 'Ah, you're the people who live in the cottage down in the copse.' Jack said. 'I've been curious about the place. You've got a fine vegetable patch there, Mr Noble.'

'Can't seem to do much with it, these days, son,' Tom Noble said. 'It needs younger muscles to do it proper justice.'

'Anytime you need a hand, you call on me,

Mr Noble,' Jack said. 'I love gardening – and veggie gardening especially.'

'I will, lad, thank you.' Tom Noble smiled.

'And you'll both always be most welcome at Skelton Castle,' Max Blaithwaite assured Mr and Mrs Noble. 'You must come up and visit little Minty, of course.'

They made their way to the kitchen, where Ellie Booth had laid on a lavish lunch. Minty swirled around her plump, pink legs, darting a happy tongue out for a lick and making Mrs Booth shriek and giggle. 'Ah, wee darling girl, you'll be wanting a bowl of something cool, I'll bet.'

Then Booth appeared in the door, a polishing cloth in his hand. Scowling glumly, he made an announcement, 'There's something strange going on in this castle, Mr Blaithwaite,' he began, wagging a warning finger. 'Ever since we came, there has been a large, red velvet cushion lying at the foot of the bed in old Miss Amelia Skelton's bedroom. Well, I was in there cleaning today – and it's gone! No trace of it. Miss Tilly, have you or either of your friends been in there and taken it?'

Tilly solemnly shook her head. 'No, Booth. Never seen it.' But Tilly looked at Mandy and

James and gave them a big, happy wink. And Mandy thought, *Wonderful, courageous Aminta.* She wouldn't be back to howl in the night in the dungeon of Skelton Castle, but, wherever she was now, she was comfortable, and at peace.

Another Hodder Children's book

CAT IN THE CRYPT
Animal Ark Hauntings 2

Lucy Daniels

Mandy and James will do anything to help an animal in distress. And sometimes even ghostly animals appear to need their help . . .

Mandy is haunted by dreams of a mysterious cat. Could it be because she is worried about Bathsheba, the vicarage tabby who has run away? Or does the strange, stone-coloured cat of her dreams have something to tell her?

ANIMAL ARK *by Lucy Daniels*

1	KITTENS IN THE KITCHEN	£3.99	❐
2	PONY IN THE PORCH	£3.99	❐
3	PUPPIES IN THE PANTRY	£3.99	❐
4	GOAT IN THE GARDEN	£3.99	❐
5	HEDGEHOGS IN THE HALL	£3.99	❐
6	BADGER IN THE BASEMENT	£3.99	❐
7	CUB IN THE CUPBOARD	£3.99	❐
8	PIGLET IN A PLAYPEN	£3.99	❐
9	OWL IN THE OFFICE	£3.99	❐
10	LAMB IN THE LAUNDRY	£3.99	❐
11	BUNNIES IN THE BATHROOM	£3.99	❐
12	DONKEY ON THE DOORSTEP	£3.99	❐
13	HAMSTER IN A HAMPER	£3.99	❐
14	GOOSE ON THE LOOSE	£3.99	❐
15	CALF IN THE COTTAGE	£3.99	❐
16	KOALA IN A CRISIS	£3.99	❐
17	WOMBAT IN THE WILD	£3.99	❐
18	ROO ON THE ROCK	£3.99	❐
19	SQUIRRELS IN THE SCHOOL	£3.99	❐
20	GUINEA-PIG IN THE GARAGE	£3.99	❐
21	FAWN IN THE FOREST	£3.99	❐
22	SHETLAND IN THE SHED	£3.99	❐
23	SWAN IN THE SWIM	£3.99	❐
24	LION BY THE LAKE	£3.99	❐
25	ELEPHANTS IN THE EAST	£3.99	❐
26	MONKEYS ON THE MOUNTAIN	£3.99	❐
27	DOG AT THE DOOR	£3.99	❐
28	FOALS IN THE FIELD	£3.99	❐
29	SHEEP AT THE SHOW	£3.99	❐
30	RACOONS ON THE ROOF	£3.99	❐
31	DOLPHIN IN THE DEEP	£3.99	❐
32	BEARS IN THE BARN	£3.99	❐
33	OTTER IN THE OUTHOUSE	£3.99	❐
34	WHALE IN THE WAVES	£3.99	❐
35	HOUND AT THE HOSPITAL	£3.99	❐
36	RABBITS ON THE RUN	£3.99	❐
37	HORSE IN THE HOUSE	£3.99	❐
38	PANDA IN THE PARK	£3.99	❐
39	TIGER ON THE TRACK	£3.99	❐
40	GORILLA IN THE GLADE	£3.99	❐
41	TABBY IN THE TUB	£3.99	❐
	SHEEPDOG IN THE SNOW	£3.99	❐
	KITTEN IN THE COLD	£3.99	❐
	FOX IN THE FROST	£3.99	❐
	HAMSTER IN THE HOLLY	£3.99	❐
	PONIES AT THE POINT	£3.99	❐
	SEAL ON THE SHORE	£3.99	❐
	ANIMAL ARK FAVOURITES	£3.99	❐
	PIGS AT THE PICNIC	£3.99	❐

All Hodder Children's books are available at your local bookshop, or can be ordered direct from the publisher. Just tick the titles you would like and complete the details below. Prices and availability are subject to change without prior notice.

Please enclose a cheque or postal order made payable to *Bookpoint Ltd*, and send to: Hodder Children's Books, 39 Milton Park, Abingdon, OXON OX14 4TD, UK. Email Address: orders@bookpoint.co.uk

If you would prefer to pay by credit card, our call centre team would be delighted to take your order by telephone. Our direct line *01235 400414* (lines open 9.00 am–6.00 pm Monday to Saturday, 24 hour message answering service). Alternatively you can send a fax on *01235 400454*.

TITLE		FIRST NAME		SURNAME	

ADDRESS	
DAYTIME TEL:	POST CODE

If you would prefer to pay by credit card, please complete:

Please debit my Visa/Access/Diner's Card/American Express (delete as applicable) card no:

Signature ....

Expiry Date: ....

If you would NOT like to receive further information on our products please tick the box. ❐